THE STALLION'S HEAD came up alertly, ears pricked, and the man Shalako opened his eyes and lay still, listening.

His guns were at hand, but he ignored them, reaching for his knife.

No sound . . . time went by, but he did not relax. Suddenly, the stallion drew back sharply and snorted. A shadow moved . . . lunged.

Shalako rolled to his knees. Unable to judge the position of the Indian in the darkness, he risked everything and slashed across in front of him, and felt the tip of the blade catch flesh. There was a muffled gasp and an iron grip seized his wrist.

Using the powerful muscles of his bent legs, Shalako straightened sharply, jerking the arm up and tearing it free. Instantly, he smashed down with a closed fist and felt it *thud* against flesh.

The Indian lunged, his knifepoint tearing Shalako's shirt. Shalako lunged in turn, missed, and the Indian seized his knife arm. . . .

Bantam Books by Louis L'Amour

SHALAKO

A NOVEL

Louis L'Amour

Postscript by Beau L'Amour

BANTAM BOOKS
NEW YORK

Shalako is a work of fiction. Names, characters, places,
and incidents are the products of the author's imagination
or are used fictitiously. Any resemblance to actual events, locales,
or persons, living or dead, is entirely coincidental.

2018 Bantam Books Mass Market Edition

Copyright © 1962 by Louis & Katherine L'Amour Trust
Postscript by Beau L'Amour © 2018 by Beau L'Amour

Published in the United States by Bantam Books, an imprint of
Random House, a division of Penguin Random House LLC, New York.

BANTAM and the HOUSE colophon are registered trademarks of
Penguin Random House LLC.

Originally published in the United States by Bantam Books,
an imprint of Random House, a division of
Penguin Random House LLC, in 1954.

ISBN 978-0-525-48632-9
Ebook ISBN 978-0-525-48640-4

Cover art: Gordon Crabb

Printed in the United States of America

randomhousebooks.com

2 4 6 8 9 7 5 3 1

Bantam Books mass market edition: December 2018

To Casey

ANIMAS MOUNTAINS
SCENE OF *SHALAKO*

Contour Intervals 100 feet

MILES

0 1 2 3 4 5

LITTLE HATCHET MOUNTAINS

SIERRA RICA

Ranch buildings

HATCHET MOUNTAINS

Hatchet Peak

Whitewater Wells

Map by William and Alan McKnight

SHALAKO

CHAPTER 1

FOR SEVEN DAYS in the spring of 1882 the man called Shalako heard no sound but the wind . . .

No sound but the wind, the creak of his saddle, the hoofbeats of his horse.

Seven days riding the ghost trails up out of Sonora, down from the Sierra Madre, through Apache country, keeping off the skylines, and watching the beckoning fingers of the talking smoke.

Lean as a famine wolf but wide and thick in the shoulder, the man called Shalako was a brooding man, a wary man, a man who trusted to no fate, no predicted destiny, nor to any luck. He trusted to nothing but his weapons, his horse, and the caution with which he rode.

His hard-boned face was tanned to saddle leather under the beat-up, black, flat-crowned hat. He wore fringed shotgun chaps, a faded red shirt, a black handkerchief knotted about his throat, and a dozen scars of knife and bullet.

It was a baked and brutal land, this Sonora, sun-blistered and arid, yet as he sifted his way through the stands of organ-pipe cactus, prickly pear and cat's claw, he knew the desert throbbed with its own strange life, and he knew those slim fingers of lifting smoke beckoned death.

He was a lone-riding man in a lonesome country, riding toward a destiny of which he knew nothing, a man who for ten long years had known no other life than this, nor wished for any other.

What else there was he had known before, but now he lived from day to day, watching the lonely sunsets flame and die, bleeding their crimson shadows against the long, serrated ridges. Watching the dawns come, seeing the mornings stir with their first life . . . and the land he rode was a land where each living thing lived by the death of some other thing.

The desert was a school, a school where each day, each hour, a final examination was offered, where failure meant death and the buzzards landed to correct the papers.

For the desert holds no easy deaths . . . hard, bitter, and ugly are the desert deaths . . . and long drawn out.

Merciless were the raw-backed mountains, dreadfully desolate the canyons, the white-faced ancient lakes were dust . . . traps where a man might die, choking horribly upon alkali or the ashen powder of ancient rocks.

For seven days Shalako heard no sound but that of his own passage, and then a gunshot bought space in the silence, a harsh whiplash of sound, followed after an instant by the shattering volley of at least four rifles.

The rifles spoke again from the sounding board of the rocks, racketing away down the canyons to fade at the desert's rim.

Motionless upon a sun-baked slope, he waited while the sweat found thin furrows through the dust on his cheeks, but there was no further sound, no further shot, nor was there movement within the range of his vision . . . merely the lazy circle of a buzzard against the heat-blurred sky.

If they had not seen him already they would not see

him if he remained still, and Shalako had learned his patience in a hard school.

Movement attracts the eye, draws the attention, renders visible. A motionless object that blends with the surroundings can long remain invisible even when close by, and Shalako was not moving.

About him lay vast, immeasurable distances, pastel shadings of salmon, pink, and lemon broken by the deeper reds of rock or the darkness of cliff shadow. Overhead the sun was lost in a copper sky above the heat-waved reaches where all sharpness of outline melted in the shimmering movement of the air.

The innocent distance that lay before him was broken by hollows, canyons, folded hills, but it seemed an even, unbroken expanse from where he sat. There were *cholla* forests out there, scatterings of lava . . . a land where anything might be and something obviously was.

The notch in the hills toward which he was pointing held a pass through the mountains, and within the pass lay a water hole.

His canteen was half-full and if necessity demanded it could be made to last another three days . . . it had done so before. In the desert a man learns to use water sparingly and to make a little cover a lot of distance.

The roan gelding was a mountain-bred horse and could survive on *cholla* or prickly pear if the spines were burned away, but water and grass lay within that opening in the hills, and Shalako had no intention of skirting the mountain unless circumstances insisted. Yet the sound of shots had come from that direction.

After a while he made, with sparing movements, a cigarette, his eyes holding on the far, blue mountains briefly, then surveying the country while he worked with the small, essential movements. He considered the possibilities, knowing that a desert offers less freedom of movement than at first seems likely. All travel in the desert, of man or animal, is governed by the need for water. Some animals learned to survive for days without water, but man was not one of these.

Four rifles . . . at least four rifles had fired that volley, and four rifles are not fired simultaneously unless fired at another man or men.

Sunset was scarcely an hour away, and the water hole was at least that far distant.

It was unlikely that whoever fired those shots would, at this hour, ride farther than the nearest water. Therefore the chances were that the water toward which he was riding would be occupied by whoever had done that shooting.

On the slope where he had drawn up neither the roan gelding nor himself would be visible at any distance, so he waited a little longer, inhaling deeply of the sharp, strong tobacco.

Four men do not fire in unison unless from ambush, and Shalako had no illusions about the sort of men who attack from concealment, nor what their attitude would be toward a drifting stranger who might have seen too much.

Whatever of gentleness lay within the man called Shalako was hidden behind the cold green eyes. There was no visible softness, no discernible shadow left by illusion. He was a man who looked upon life with a dispassionate, wry realism.

He knew he lived by care and by chance, knowing the next man he met might be the man who would kill him, or the next mile might see his horse down with a broken leg . . . and a man without a horse in this country was two-thirds a dead man.

To his thinking those men who thought their hour was predestined were fools. Whatever else nature was, it was impersonal, inexorable. He had seen too much of death to believe it was important, too much of life to believe that the destiny of any creature was important to any but itself or those dependent upon it.

There was always life. Humans and animals and plants were born and died, they lived their brief hour and went their way, their places filled so quickly they were scarcely missed.

Only the mountains lasted, and even they changed. Their lasting was only an idea in the minds of men because they lasted a little longer than men. Shalako knew he would live as long as he moved with care, considered the possibilities, and kept out of line of any stray bullet. Yet he was without illusions; for all his care, death could come and suddenly.

The margin for error was slight. A dry water hole, a chance fall, a stray bullet . . . or an Apache he missed seeing first.

Those who talked of a bullet with their name on it were fools . . . to a bullet all targets were anonymous.

Behind him to the east lay Mexico, but what trail he left back there only an Apache or a wolf might follow. Deliberately, he had avoided all known water holes, keeping to the roughest country, seeking out the rarely used seeps or *tinajas,* and avoiding the places an Apache might go in search of food.

He had seen nobody in those seven days, and nobody had seen him. He was quite sure of that for, had he been seen, he would be dead. Yet he knew that the Apaches had come down out of the Sierra Madre and were riding north.

He read the story in those weird hieroglyphics of the desert, the trails of unshod ponies, deserted rancherias, faint dust trails hanging above the desert, and always of course, the talking smoke.

Holding to the seeps and the natural tanks as he had, he had been fairly safe. Such places were rarely used except when the year was far along or it was a dry season. Early in the spring the desert water holes were full and there was no need to stray from them.

Removing his hat, he wiped the sweatband. No further sounds had reached him, nor was there any dust. Around him the desert lay still as on the day the earth was born. Yet he did not move.

Big Hatchet Peak towered more than eight thousand feet just to the south and west. He had crossed the border from Mexico into the States at a point in the foothills of the Sierra Rica, knowing the approximate location of the water hole toward which he was riding.

It lay about two miles up a canyon and two trails led from it. One started south and east, then swung westward toward Whitewater Wells, every inch of it Apache country.

The second trail was dim, scarcely used even by Indians, an ancient trail that dated back to the Mimbres people, long vanished from their old haunts, if not from the face of the earth.

This trail led almost due west from the water hole, was much shorter and less likely to be watched. The mind of the man called Shalako, as of most Western men, was a storehouse of such information. Where guidebooks and maps are not available, every campfire, chuck wagon, and saloon bar becomes a clearinghouse for information.

It was hot, and the roan was streaked with sweat and dust. The border country can be cool in April. It can also be an oven, the way it was now.

He started his horse, walking it to keep the dust down. From the shade of a nearby boulder an irritable rattler buzzed unpleasantly, and then for a time a chaparral cock raced ahead of him, enjoying the company.

He paused again by a clump of ironwood, enjoying the fragrance from the yellow blossoms of some nearby cat's claw. Sometimes called "wait-a-minute," it was a low, spreading shrub with peculiar hooklike thorns that had crippled many a horse or other animal.

His eyes studied the desert. The tracks of a small lizard were visible in the sand . . . bees hummed around the cat's-claw blossoms. Shadows were beginning to thicken in some of the far-off canyons, although the sun was still high.

Shalako continued to walk his horse forward, and each time he mounted a slope, he came up easily at the crest until only his head showed above the hill, and there, holding very still to simulate a rock, he allowed only his eyes to move until he had scanned the area within view.

After almost an hour of slow progress, he rode down a draw toward a small playa, or dry lake. It was unlikely the killers had remained in the area but Shalako was not a trusting man.

Within the mouth of the draw he drew rein again. With his first glance he recognized the body for what it was, but only when he was quite sure that he was alone did he approach it. He circled it as warily as a wolf, studying it from all angles, and when finally he stopped within a dozen feet of the dead man he knew much of what had happened at this place.

The dead man had ridden a freshly shod horse into the playa from the north, and when shot he had tumbled from the saddle and the horse had galloped away. Several riders on unshod ponies had then approached the body and one had dismounted to collect the weapons.

The clothing had not been stripped off, nor was the body mutilated. Only when he could learn no more by observation did he dismount and turn the body over. He was already sure of the dead man's identity.

Pete Wells . . .

An occasional scout for the Army, a sometime driver of freight wagons, a former buffalo hunter and lately a hanger-on around Fort Bowie, Fort Grant, or Tucson. A man of no particular quality, honest enough, and not a man likely to make enemies. Yet now he was dead, shot from ambush.

Circling, Shalako discovered where the ambushers had lain in wait.

Four men . . . four Apaches.

He studied the droppings of the horses, kicking them apart with a boot toe. He recognized in those droppings seeds from a plant found in the foothills of the Sierra Madre, but not farther north.

These were not reservation Indians from San Carlos then, they were some of Chato's outfit, just up from below the border.

Their trail when they left Wells's body lay in the direction he himself was taking, and that meant the water hole was off-limits for Shalako unless he wished to fight them for it, and no man in his right mind started a fight with Apaches.

When the time came for fighting, the man Shalako fought with a cold fury that had an utterly impersonal quality about it. He fought to win, fought with deadly efficiency, with no nonsense about him, yet he did not fight needlessly.

Despite his weariness and that of his horse he began backtracking the dead man.

Pete Wells was not likely to be alone, so his presence indicated a camp nearby, and a camp meant water. Yet Shalako puzzled over his presence here at such a time.

The Hatchet Mountains were in a corner of New Mexico that projected somewhat south of the rest of the state line. It was a desert and mountain region, off the main trails and offering no inducements to travel except several routes into Mexico. These were routes used by the Apaches in making their raids, but by no one else.

Unless Wells had been with the Army.

Within a few minutes Shalako knew that was highly unlikely, for Wells had been following another rider or looking for someone whom he did not fear. Wells had mounted every ridge and knoll to survey the surrounding country, and Wells knew better than to take such risks.

Obviously, he knew nothing of the movement of the Apaches, and that implied that nobody else knew as yet. Wells was close to the Army and would be among the first to hear.

Shalako had backtrailed Wells for less than two miles when he came upon the trail Wells had lost.

Pausing briefly, Shalako tried to form a picture of the situation, for to follow a trail successfully it is first necessary to know something of the motives of the person followed.

Both horses were freshly shod, and both moved with an eagerness that implied they had come but a short distance.

Wells was no such tracker as Shalako, a fact Wells would have been the first to admit and, swinging a wide circle, Shalako picked up the lost trail in a matter of minutes.

What he found was merely a white scratch . . . the scar of an iron shoe upon a rock. Farther along a bit of stepped-on sage, then a partial hoof track almost hidden by a creosote bush. The trail led toward the Hatchet Mountains and, judging by the crushed sage, it was no more than two hours old.

By the time, some thirty minutes later, that he was riding up the slope that led to the base of the Hatchets, he knew a good deal more about the person he was following. He also knew why Wells had been following and that there was a fairly large camp in the vicinity.

In the first place, the rider was in no hurry, and was unfamiliar with the country. As there were no inhabited ranches or mines in the area, this implied a camp close enough for the rider to return before dark.

Here and there the rider had paused to look more closely at things, interesting enough in themselves, but too familiar for a Western man to notice.

At one point the rider had attempted to pick the blossom from a prickly pear. The blossom lay where it had been hastily dropped. Shalako's face broke into a sudden grin that brought a surprising warmth to his bleak features.

Whoever plucked that blossom had a bunch of stickers in her fingers.

Her?

Yes, he was sure the rider was a girl or woman. The tracks of the horse, for example . . . it was a horse of medium build with a good stride . . . the tracks were but lightly pressed upon the sand, which implied a rider of no great weight.

Moreover, Pete Wells had been extremely anxious to find the rider, which also implied a woman about whom he was worried. He might have followed any tenderfoot, but a man like Wells, almost any Western man in fact, would have the feeling that whatever a man did was his own problem.

If a man was big enough to make his own tracks and carry a gun, he was a responsible person, responsible for himself and his actions, and not to be pampered.

A man in the Western lands was as big as he wanted to be, and as good or as bad as he wished. What law existed was local law and it felt no responsibility for the actions of any man when they took place out of its immediate jurisdiction. There were very few borderline cases. Men were good and bad . . . simply that . . . the restrictions were few, the chances of concealment almost nonexistent. A man who was bad was boldly bad, and nobody sheltered or protected any man.

But this rider was a woman, of that Shalako was now sure.

The horse the woman rode was a mare . . . back there a short way the rider had drawn up to look over the country and the mare took the occasion to respond to a call of nature . . . from the position of her feet it was obvious she was a mare.

Men in the West rarely rode mares or stallions. There might be exceptions, but they were so scarce as to attract a good deal of attention. They rode geldings because they were less trouble among other horses.

Suddenly, almost in the shadow of the mountains, he saw where a trail of unshod ponies had crossed ahead of him. The rider he followed had noticed them also.

"One up for her," he said aloud. "At least she has her eyes open."

The rider had drawn up, the mare dancing nervously, eager to be moving.

Now he scored another mark for the rider . . . a tenderfoot and a woman, but no damned fool . . . she had turned abruptly north and, skirting a nest of boulders, had entered a canyon. That last was not a good move but, obviously alarmed, she was seeking the quickest route back to camp.

The roan stumbled often now and Shalako drew rein beside the boulders and got down. Pouring a little water into his bandanna, he squeezed the last drop into the roan's mouth. He did this several times, and was about to step back into the saddle when he heard a horse's hoof click on stone.

He swung his leg over the saddle, then stood in the stirrups to look over the top of the boulder.

Evidently the canyon had proved impassable or a dead end, for the rider was returning. And the rider was a woman.

Not only a woman, but a young woman, and a beautiful woman.

How long since he had seen a girl like that? Shalako watched her ride toward him, noting the ease with which she rode, the grace of manner, the immaculate clothing.

A lady, this one. She was from a world that he had almost forgotten . . . bit by bit his memories had faded behind the blazing suns, the hot, still valleys, the raw-backed hills.

She rode a sorrel, and she rode sidesaddle, her gray riding skirt draped gracefully over the side of the mare, and she rode with the ease of long practice. Yet he was grimly pleased to see the businesslike way her rifle came up when he appeared from around the rock. He had no doubt that she would shoot if need be. Moreover, he suspected she would be a very good shot.

She drew up a dozen yards away, but if she was frightened there was no visible evidence of it.

"None of my business, but this here is Apache country."

"So?"

"You know a man named Pete Wells?"

"Yes. He's our wagon master."

"Pete never did have much sense." He gathered his reins. "Lady, you'd better get back to your camp wherever it is and tell them to pack up and hightail it out of here."

"Why should I do a thing like that?"

"I think you've guessed," he said, "I think you had an idea when you saw those tracks back yonder." He gestured to indicate the mountains far behind him. Their near flank was shadowed now, but the crest carried a crown of gold from the sun's bright setting. "Over there in the Sierra Rica there's an Apache named Chato. He just rode up out of Mexico with a handful of warriors, and here and there some others are riding to meet him. He will soon be meeting with some more who have jumped their reservation, and within forty-eight hours there won't be a man or woman alive in this corner of New Mexico."

"We have been looking forward to meeting some Indians," she replied coolly. "Frederick has been hoping for a little brush with them."

"Your Frederick is a damned fool."

"I should advise you not to say that to him."

Shalako handed her his field glass. "Over east there. See that smoke? Over by the peak?"

"I see nothing."

"Keep looking."

She moved the glass, searching against the far-off, purpling mountains. Suddenly, the glass ceased to move. "Oh? You mean that thin column of smoke?"

"It's a talking smoke . . . the telegraph of the Apache. You and your outfit better light out fast. You already got one man killed."

"I . . . *what?*"

"Pete was always a damn fool, but even he should have known better than to bring a party of greenhorns into this country at a time like this."

Her cheeks paled. "Are you telling me that Pete Wells is dead?"

"We've sat here too long. Let's get out of here."

"Why should I be responsible? I mean, if he is dead?"

"He's dead, all right. If he hadn't been skylining himself on every hill while hunting for you he might not have been seen."

He led off along the base of the Hatchets, heading north. The gaunt land was softening with shadows, but was somehow increasingly lonely. The girl turned in her saddle to look toward the distant finger of smoke, and suddenly she shivered.

"We're at a ranch north of the range," she told him. "Mr. Wells took us there. The place is deserted."

"How'd you get in here past the troops?"

"Frederick did not want an official escort. He wished to see the Apache in battle."

"Any man who hunts Apache trouble is a child."

Her tone was cool. "You do not understand. Frederick is a soldier. He was a general in the Franco-Prussian War when he was twenty-five. He was a national hero."

"We had one of those up north a few years back. His name was Custer."

Irritated by his amused contempt, she made no reply for several minutes yet, despite her anger with him, she was observant enough to note that he rode with caution, never ceased to listen, and his eyes were always busy. She had hunted before this, and her father had hunted, and she had seen the Masai hunt in Africa . . . they were like this man now.

"It is silly to think that naked savages could oppose modern weapons. Frederick is amused by all the trouble your Army seems to have."

He looked uneasily into the evening. There was a warning in the stillness. Like a wild thing he felt strange premonitions, haunting feelings of danger. He felt it now. Unknowingly he looked eastward toward the mountains, unknowingly because upon a ridge of those mountains an Apache looked westward . . . miles lay between them.

Tats-ah-das-ay-go, the Quick-Killer, Apache warrior feared even by his own people . . . master of all the wiles, the deceits, the skills. He looked westward now, wondering.

At the no longer deserted ranch where the hunting party of Baron Frederick von Hallstatt built its cooking fires, a man beside one of the fires suddenly stood up and looked away from the fire.

He was a lean and savage man with a boy's soft beard along his jaws, high cheekbones, and a lantern jaw. His thin neck lifted from a greasy shirt collar, and he looked into the distance as if he had heard a sound out there. The .44 Colt on his thigh was a deadly thing.

Bosky Fulton was a gunman who had never heard of either *Tats-ah-das-ay-go* or Shalako Carlin. He did not know that his life was already bound inextricably to those two and to the girl Irina, whom he did know. Yet the night made him restless.

Back upon the desert, Shalako had drawn up in a cluster of ocotillo clumps and under their slight cover he studied the country around, choosing a way.

"Every Apache," he said conversationally, "knows all your Frederick knows about tactics before he is twelve, and they learn it the hard way. The desert is their field of operations and they know its every phase and condition. Every operation your Frederick learned in a book or on a blackboard they learned in battle. And they have no base to protect, no supply line to worry about."

"How do they eat?"

He swept a gesture at the surrounding desert. "You can't see them but there are a dozen food plants within sight, and a half dozen that are good for medicine."

The sun brushed the sky with reflected rose and with arrows of brightest gold. The serrated ridges caught belated glory . . . out upon the desert a quail called inquiringly.

She felt obliged to defend their attitude. "There are eight of us, and we are accompanied by four scouts or hunters, eight teamsters, two cooks, and two skinners. We have eight wagons."

"That explains something that's been bothering me. The Apaches started eating their horses two days ago."

"*Eating* them?"

"Only thing an Apache likes better than horse meat is mule meat. He will ride a horse until it's half dead and, when they find a place where they can get more horses, they will eat those they have."

"You are implying they expect to have our horses?"

The desert was too still, and it worried him. He got down from the saddle and rinsed his bandanna once more in the roan's mouth. As she watched him the girl's anger went out of her.

She looked at him again, surprised at the softness in his eyes and the gentleness with which he handled the horse.

"You love your horse."

"Horse is like a woman. Keep a strong hand on the bridle and pet 'em a mite and they'll stand up to most anything. Just let 'em get the bit in their teeth and they'll make themselves miserable and a man, too."

"Women are not animals."

"Matter of viewpoint."

"Some women don't want a master."

"Those are the miserable ones. Carry their heads high and talk about independence. Seems to me an independent woman is a lonely woman."

"You are independent, are you not?"

"Different sort of thing. The sooner women realize that men are different, the better off they'll be. The more independent a woman becomes the less of a woman she is, and the less of a woman she is the less she is of anything worthwhile."

"I don't agree."

"Didn't figure on it. A woman shouldn't try to be like a man. Best she can be is a poor imitation and nobody wants anything but the genuine article.

"Nature intended woman to keep a home and a hearth. Man is a hunter, a rover . . . sometimes he has to go far afield to make a living, so it becomes his nature."

He kept his voice low and without thinking of it she had done the same.

"And where is your woman?"

"Don't have one."

The sun was gone when they reached the last rocky point of the Hatchets. About a mile away a tall peak thrust up from the desert and beyond were a couple of lesser peaks, and still farther the distant bulk of the Little Hatchets. West of the nearest peak was a dark blotch of ranch buildings, and among them some spots of white that could be wagon covers. And in their midst blazed a fire, too large a fire.

Smelling water, the roan tugged at the bit, but there was a feeling in the air that Shalako did not like.

They sat still, while he listened into the night, feeling its uneasiness. It was not quite dark, although the stars were out. The desert was visible, the dark spots of brush and cacti plainly seen.

Into the silence she said, "I am Irina Carnarvon."

She said it as one says a name that should be known, but he did not for the time place the name, for he was a man to whom names had ceased to matter.

"My name is Carlin . . . they call me Shalako."

He started the roan down the gentle slope. The roan was too good a horse to lose and in no shape to run, but the ranch was safety and the ranch was two miles off. He slid his rifle from its scabbard.

"Get ready to run. We'll walk our horses as far as we can, but once we start running, pay me no mind. You just ride the hell out of here."

"Your horse is in no shape to run."

"My problem."

The roan quickened his pace. There was a lot of stuff in that roan, a lot of stuff.

"You *actually* believe we are in danger?"

"You people are a pack of idiots. Right now you and that tin-braided general of yours are in more trouble than you ever saw before."

"You are not polite."

"I've no time for fools."

Anger kept her silent, yet she sensed the uneasiness of her horse and it made her wary. A fine horsewoman, she knew the feeling at once and it frightened her far more than the warnings of the stranger.

Silence, and the distant fire . . . the hoof falls of the horses . . . the stars against the soft darkness of the sky, the loom of mountains . . . a coolness in the air, balm after the day's fierce heat. The quickening pace of the horses, the faint gleam along the rifle barrel. A slight breeze touched her cheek.

"Shalako . . . it is a strange name."

"Name of the Zuni rain god. Seemed like every time I showed up in their country it rained, so they called me that for a joke."

"I did not realize Indians had a sense of humor."

"The greatest. Nobody has more humor than an Indian, and I know. I've lived among them."

"I heard they were so stoical."

"Indians act that way around white men they don't

know because they don't want to answer a lot of fool questions."

They were out of the flat now, at least a quarter of a mile gained.

The Apache, in distinction from many other Indians, preferred not to fight at night, believing the soul of a warrior killed at such a time must wander forever in darkness. That did not mean that on occasion an Apache would not take a chance.

When the camp was less than a mile away and they could hear faint sounds, an Apache suddenly raised up from behind a greasewood bush with a bowstring drawn back . . . but he had stood up directly in front of the muzzle of Shalako's rifle and less than thirty feet off.

He heard the *thud* of the bullet into flesh in the instant the arrow whizzed past his ear.

Startled by the explosion of the gunshot, both horses leaped into a run. Behind them there was another shot and Shalako felt the bullet when it struck the cantle of his saddle and caromed off into the night.

The roan ran proudly, desperately, determined not to lose the race to the fresher horse. A wave of fierce pride swept over Shalako and he realized again the unconquerable spirit of the roan mustang.

Neck and neck they raced for the ranch, and Shalako let go with a wild Texas yell to warn those ahead that he was not a charging Indian.

On a dead run they swept into the ranch yard and drew up in a cloud of swirling dust. Several people started toward them, and Shalako glanced sharply around, taking in the camp and those who peopled it with that one sweeping glance.

The man who walked up to them first was tall. He

was lean and strong, with blond hair and handsome, if somewhat cold, features. His eyes were white gray, his boots polished and immaculate, his white shirt crisp and clean.

"What happened? Did you see a coyote?" His eyes went from Irina to Shalako, taking in his dusty, travel-worn clothing, his battered hat, and unshaved face.

"Better circle your wagons into the gaps between the buildings," Shalako suggested. "Get your stock inside the circle. That was an Apache, not a coyote."

The gray eyes turned again to Shalako, cool, atten-tive. "There are no Indians off the reservations," the blond man said. "Our man Wells told us—"

"Your man Wells is dead. If you want him you'll find him all spraddled out in a dry lake southeast of here, as full of holes as a prairie dog town . . . and it wasn't any reservation Indian who shot him."

"Who is this man, Irina?"

"Mr. Carlin, the Baron Frederick von Hallstatt."

"If you want to live," Shalako said, "forget the for-malities."

Von Hallstatt ignored the remark. "Thank you for bringing Lady Carnarvon back to camp, Carlin. Now if you want something to eat, just go to the cook and tell him I sent you."

"Thanks, but I'm not staying that long. This outfit doesn't have a prayer and I'm not going down the chute with it. I'm riding out."

"Your pleasure," von Hallstatt replied coolly, and lifted a hand to help Irina from the saddle.

Two of the men who had come forward were standing by, and one of them said, "Forget it, General. This fellow was scared by a shadow."

The roan gelding swung as of its own volition and faced the speaker. Shalako's face was half-hidden by the pulled-down brim of his hat, but what the man could see he did not like. "Mister"—Shalako's voice was utterly cold—"I saw Apaches out there. What I shot was an Apache. Do you want to call me a liar?"

The man backed off a step. Desperately, he wanted to call the name and draw his gun, but something about the man on the roan horse made him hesitate.

"None of that!" Von Hallstatt's voice rang with the harshness of command. "Carlin, we thank you for escorting Lady Carnarvon back to camp. Eat if you wish. Sleep here if you wish, but I suggest you be gone by daybreak."

"By daybreak you'll be fighting for your lives. I'll be gone within the hour."

Turning away from them he rode the roan to the water tank. An ambitious settler had built this tank before the Apaches canceled out his faith in humanity by putting a half-dozen arrows in his belly.

He had been a sincere man, a good man. He believed that he who planted a tree or dug a well was closest to God, and would be blessed by all who needed water, or needed shade.

He also believed, good trusting man, that if he was himself peaceful others would be peaceful toward him.

He did not realize that others operate by a different philosophy and to those peace is unrealistic. Nor did he know that to an Apache all who are not of his tribe are enemies, that kindness was to them a sign of weakness.

He was, nevertheless, a man of stamina as well as faith, and he lasted for three days, the arrows in his belly, tied head down to a wagon wheel, close to water but unable to reach it . . . and all this under a blazing summer sun.

He left no record of his philosophy at the end of that time.

Shalako allowed the roan to drink sparingly, then drew him back from the water and, stripping off the saddle, rubbed the horse down with a handful of dry grass, and as he worked his eyes took in the disposition of the camp.

He had never seen anything like it. The wagons were scattered haphazardly about, the teamsters loafing around a smaller fire, von Hallstatt's companions dressed as if for a hunt in England or Virginia, served by a chef in a white apron and chef's hat.

No effort had been made to prepare for attack, all was elaborately casual, with much conversation and laughter.

The stable was the sturdiest-looking building, close to the water tank, and with a lower story of adobe, an upper story of hewn logs. There were several narrow ports for firing. The stable was built much like an old-fashioned blockhouse.

The house had been built at a much later date and by the peace-loving settler, and offered no practical defenses. Nor did the sheds and outbuildings. Yet they did form a rough rectangle with the house at the east end and the stable on the south. By drawing wagons into the gaps between the buildings the area could be made a fortress against any ordinary attack, with a final retreat to the stable in a last emergency.

Suddenly a sound of approaching steps made him look up. "*Shalako!* I'll be damned! Where'd you blow in from?"

Shalako straightened wearily, dropping the grass. "Buffalo? This is a long way from Fort Griffin." He dusted fragments of dry grass from his fingers. "Me? From the Sierra Madre, riding neck and neck with Chato and about forty Apaches. At least, there'll be forty of them by now."

"You ain't foolin'?"

"I'm riding out tonight."

Buffalo Harris swore bitterly. "An' the Army doesn't even know we're in the Territory! Was that you who shot out there awhile back?"

Shalako indicated the cantle of his saddle. "Feel of that . . . fired from off at the side or it might have taken me right out of the saddle."

Buffalo laid a finger in the groove and whistled softly. "They don't come much closer."

"How'd you ever tie up with a haywire outfit like this?"

"Haywire? Are you crazy? This here is the most fixed-up outfit I ever seen! They got champagne, crab, oysters . . . everything. She's a mighty plush setup, Shalako, an' don't you forget it . . . and the best grub I ever eat."

"So you lose your hair. Saddle up and come with me."

"Can't do it. I told them I stay the route."

Von Hallstatt strode up and, seeing Buffalo, stopped. "Harris, do you know this man?"

Buffalo spat. "I know him. He was scoutin' for the Army when he was sixteen. Knows more about this country than the Apaches do."

"Then you should go to work for me, Carlin. I can use a good man."

"If you don't pull those wagons into position you won't be in shape to hire anybody. Chato started eating his spare horses two, three days ago, which means they planned to steal yours before they crossed the border."

"That's impossible. They could not have known we were here."

"They knew . . . they knew you have four women with you, how many horses and mules you have, and how many men. No, I'm riding out of here."

Yet, even as he said it, he knew the roan was in no shape for an all-night ride . . . or a ride anywhere, for that matter. The mustang needed rest, food, and water.

Nevertheless, he was getting out. These people had come there under their own power, they could get out the same way.

Von Hallstatt measured Shalako with cool eyes. He disliked the man, this he admitted. On the other hand, someone who knew the country as well as Buffalo said he did might be useful. Especially with Wells dead, if, of course, he was dead.

"If you would name your price, Carlin, we would like to have you with us." He took his pipe from between his teeth. "You might at least stay and see the fun."

"You're not going to be having any fun." Shalako was brusque. "Unless you're shot with luck every man jack of you will be dead within forty-eight hours."

Von Hallstatt laughed. "Oh, come now! Naked savages against modern weapons?"

On a beat-up horse his chances of survival were slight, but this camp had the mark of death upon it, and realization that he had no choice but to make a run for it made Shalako increasingly irritable.

"Mister, let me tell you a little story about a West Pointer we had named Fetterman. He used to make his brag that given eighty men he could ride through the whole Sioux nation. Fetterman was well trained, he was efficient, and he was bulging at the seams with all those fancy European tactics, and he was confident.

"One day they sent him out with eighty men to rescue some wagons that were under attack, and they warned him if the Indians ran, not to chase them.

"He had his eighty men and his chance, and he chased them. His eighty men lasted less than twenty minutes, less time than you'd take to drink a cup of hot coffee, actually."

Shalako began to build a smoke. "Do you know how they did it? Like Hannibal at the Battle of Cannae . . . the center fell back and, when Fetterman followed them in, the flanks closed around him and wiped him out."

"You would have me believe these savages understand tactics?"

"Unless I miss the breed, you'll be from one of the old Junker families of Prussia. War has been a way of life to you for centuries, yet I doubt if you have seen more than ten battles, or that your oldest general has seen more than thirty."

Shalako folded the paper over his cigarette. "Mister, out there in the dark there are forty or fifty Apaches and the chances are there isn't one of them who isn't a veteran of fifty to a hundred battles. They fight Americans, Mexicans, other Indians. War is a way of life for the Apache, too, and every child learns his tactics by listening to the warriors talk of their battles.

"There isn't a thing in Vegetius, Saxe, or Jomini an Indian doesn't know, and more besides. He is the greatest guerrilla fighter the world has ever known.

"He doesn't know a thing about all that military balderdash of close-order drill, military courtesy, or parade-ground soldiering. Everything he learns is by applying it that way. He's taught, sure, but he's taught to fight and to win and he wastes time on none of the fixings.

"You boys say close-order drill is good for discipline. That's nonsense. The only kind of discipline that counts is the discipline of training to function in battle. How to keep in touch with the men on either side of you, how to advance and retreat under fire, how to give covering fire and supporting fire, how to select routes of travel under risk of attack. You don't learn any of that training for a lot of parade-ground nonsense.

"There isn't a thing to learn about fighting in this country—and this is the worst country in the world to fight in—that every Apache out there doesn't know."

"I am surprised," von Hallstatt said contemptuously, "that your Army is able to defeat these supermen of yours. These super-Indians."

"I'll tell you why. Only one out of three or four has a rifle, and he may not have a dozen rounds of ammunition. Unless they can find a crooked trader to supply them they have to kill to get weapons, so they are always in short supply.

"And the Army outnumbers them fifty-to-one. And that Army is the best bunch of fighting men the sun ever shone on. They use Indian tactics part of the time themselves, and General Crook, who knew more about fighting Indians than any of them, he used Indians to fight them."

Shalako turned toward the fire. "And let me tell you something else: Any rattle-headed fool who would bring a bunch of women into a country like this at a time like this deserves to be shot."

Deliberately, he turned his back and walked away toward the fire where he glanced at the coffeepot, then walked on to the stable where he filled a feed bag and carried it back to the roan. The feed bag was alien but the oats were not. After a little hesitation and backing away the roan decided to accept the situation.

Von Hallstatt had walked away, but Harris was still there.

"That was medicine talk, but the general was sure sore." Harris watched while Shalako picked up his rifle. "What happened to Pete?"

Shalako explained, then jerked his head toward von Hallstatt. "Is he carrying money?"

"You ain't just a-woofin'! And diamonds? These women are wearin' diamonds like they were candy! And you should see their rifles and shotguns! Inlaid with gold, ivory and mother-of-pearl. I d'clare, Shalako, these folks must have a fortune in guns."

"Then I know why Rio Hockett is here."

"Where'd you know him?"

"The Rangers chased him out of the brush down on the Nueces a few years ago. He's been a horse thief, a cow rustler, and a scalp hunter. If you folks get out of here alive, you talk von Hallstatt into getting rid of him. He's trouble."

Buffalo was silent for several minutes, and then he said, "You don't think we've got a chance, do you?"

"With Chato and forty Apaches out there? What do you think?"

Irina Carnarvon came suddenly from the darkness with a plate of food and a cup of coffee. "You must be starved, Mr. Carlin."

Buffalo Harris faded discreetly into the shadows and Shalako reached for the food gratefully. The very smell of it made him faint, he was that hungry. He had run out of jerked meat—the last food he had—the day before yesterday and had not dared chance a shot, although he had seen a couple of deer.

Irina stood beside him, and the faint smell of her perfume stirred old memories. He glanced at her over his coffee cup. She was tall for a woman, slender but rounded . . . quite a woman.

His eyes went beyond her to the tables that were being spread with white linen and set with silver and sparkling glassware. He shook his head in amazement to see such a thing in New Mexico, with Apaches around the camp.

There was a low murmur of conversation from a group of people who sat in camp chairs near the fire. It was the polite conversation of well-bred people everywhere, idle, interesting talk, but strangely incongruous here.

"What are you doing with this outfit?" he asked bluntly. "You're real."

She turned to look at him. "They are real, too, Mr. Carlin. It is merely another sort of life."

"But unreal here, and unrealistic. That sort of thing is fine in England, or New England. Out here, at a time like this it reminds me of Nero's fiddle."

"You asked me what I was doing here. These are my friends, Mr. Carlin . . . and I may marry Frederick."

It irritated her that she hesitated before saying it, almost as if she were ashamed, which she certainly was not. In the East and in Europe, almost everywhere in fact, Frederick von Hallstatt was considered quite a catch. His was an ancient family, he had won many honors in the Prussian Army, he had a title, position, and wealth.

He put down the plate. "Men must be mighty scarce where you come from."

"Most people believe that I am fortunate."

He glanced at her. "You are warm, friendly, and I think sentimental," Shalako said. "He is cold, calculating, and ruthless. Furthermore," he added, "he's a fool, or he would never have brought you here."

"You make up your mind very quickly," she spoke stiffly. "I am not sure you are qualified to render an opinion."

"Out here we don't have time to consider folks. We have to make up our minds fast, and we judge a man by his looks and his actions. We pay no attention to titles or honors or whatever because we have found they don't measure a man. Yes, I made a fast judgment on him, and I may be wrong."

"I think you are very wrong."

"I don't believe you," he said. "You're too smart a girl to make a mistake like that."

This man was a total stranger, a big, unshaved, and rugged man out of the desert. Very likely he had not bathed in a week . . . where he would get the water she could not imagine . . . and she was discussing her friends with him. It was preposterous.

His thoughts had moved into the darkness, thinking beyond this place, thinking of the trail westward. The roan was in no shape, but if he could get over into the Animas Mountains he might hole up and rest for a while, then move out and keep to low ground.

"Come with me," he said suddenly, "and I'll get you out of this."

"And leave my friends? You must be mad." She paused. "I scarcely know you, Mr. Carlin, and I could never leave my friends if they are in as much danger as you assume."

He was scarcely listening, his mind was out upon the desert, thinking of the way that lay before him. He owed these people nothing, and this was a country where a man saddled his own broncs and fought his own battles. They had come into the country recklessly, foolishly, hoping for a "brush with the Apaches" . . . well, they would get it.

"You must take one of my horses, Mr. Carlin. I have three, very fine horses, and your horse is half-dead."

"You'd swap?"

"Certainly not. But I will loan him to you, and when you can, return him and pick up your own horse. If you are correct and we do not get out of here, you may keep him."

"You needn't do this, you know. You owe me nothing."

She looked up at him. "I wasn't thinking of you, Mr. Carlin. I was remembering what you said about them eating their horses. I couldn't bear them eating Mohammet."

He chuckled suddenly. "Now I like that. You're honest, anyway. All right, I'll take care of your horse."

She turned abruptly and walked away, and he stared after her, aware of a feeling of guilt. In a few minutes Harris returned, leading a stallion.

Black as midnight, he knew at once that he had never seen a horse to compare with it. Clean-limbed and strong, it was built both for speed and staying power. When he reached for the stallion it thrust a velvety nose into his palm.

He talked to the horse, rubbing its neck and making friends.

"You must have put the sign on that girl, Shalako. This is her best horse, and she treats it like a child. Pure Arab, right out of the desert."

He threw his saddle on the stallion and cinched it up, and the stallion took the bit eagerly, as if he was eager to go. Shalako had known such horses, as excited about a trail as a man would be.

Buffalo Harris left, and when he returned he had a small packet of food. Shalako took his time, reluctant to leave now that a way was open.

Von Hallstatt had given the order and the wagons had been pulled into the spaces between the buildings, making a fairly tight circle. It was too large to defend well, yet it could be defended, and there were quite a few men, all well-armed.

As Shalako put his blanket roll behind the saddle, someone behind him spoke.

"What you all figure to do with that horse?"

Shalako turned slowly.

The man facing him was lean and narrow-shouldered, a sparse beard on his jaws. Bosky Fulton was a trouble-hunting man, and Shalako read him at a glance, nor was he inclined to sidestep it. Shalako knew all too well that any sign of hesitation would be accepted as a sign of fear.

"None of your damned business," he said coldly, and as he spoke he stepped closer to Fulton.

Few gunmen could stand up to a close fight. Most of them fancied their shooting ability, but at close range there was too much chance of both men being killed . . . and no man wants to die.

Fulton backed off a step, to keep the distance between them, but Shalako followed. "None of your business," Shalako said coldly.

Fulton stared hard at Shalako, thinking to intimidate him, but the eyes that looked back into his showed only contempt, and something else that Fulton liked even less.

Before Fulton could speak, Harris interrupted. "Lady Carnarvon loaned him the horse, Bosky. It's all right."

"*Loaned* him?" Fulton was incredulous. "She won't even let anybody touch him."

Frederick von Hallstatt walked up; he ignored Fulton, but glanced from the horse to Shalako. "Lady Carnarvon loaned you that horse?" he asked doubtfully. "I can't believe it."

Laura Davis and Irina had also come up. "Yes, I loaned Mohammet to him, Frederick. I believe if we are attacked he will be safer with Mr. Carlin than with us."

"Attacked? You believe that story, then?"

"You forget, Frederick. I was out there with him. Those shots were very real."

"If you can get out of here," Shalako suggested, "make a run for it to Fort Cummings. Lieutenant Colonel Forsyth is in command there."

He lingered, reluctant to leave. "You get your grub and ammunition inside the stable. They'll be all around you, come daylight, and you won't see any of them.

"The way I read the smokes, Indians have left the reservation to join Chato, and that means the Army will have been notified and Forsyth will be out. If you burn your wagons the Army will be likely to see the smoke."

"I doubt if it will come to that," von Hallstatt replied.

"We have a good-sized force and we are well-armed. And several of us have had military experience."

"No matter what experience you've had, in this kind of war you're a tenderfoot." Shalako gathered the reins. "Thanks, ma'am, and good luck. You're quite a woman."

He walked the Arab into the darkness near the stable and drew up to listen, shutting out the sounds of the camp to hear only the desert.

There was an eagerness in the stallion. The Arab liked the feel of the night and the desert, and no doubt some forgotten or atavistic memory stirred his Arab blood on such desert nights as this.

Ears pricked, dainty as a dancer, the black Arab moved down into the wash, holding close to the near bank and the deepest shadow.

His hoofs made no sound in the soft sand, and for several minutes they went cautiously forward, but soon Shalako sensed that something lay to the north that the Arab did not like. Shalako let the horse pull away to the south a little, trusting the horse had caught the scent of an Apache.

Westward, eight or nine miles away, lay the Animas Mountains, an area he knew better than the Hatchets, and a place where he knew of a hideout where with luck he might hole up. Yet the farther he rode the more irritable he became.

The wind was in his face . . . he smelled dust.

Quickly he drew the Arab into the deepest shadow, whispering to him to quiet his excitement.

And then he heard a sound . . . the soft scuffle of hoofs in the sand.

A party of riders coming from the northwest, and they

would be coming down into the wash somewhere close to him.

Shalako drew his Colt and rested the barrel on the saddle horn. The night was still and cool, the sound of hoofs was closer now, like surf upon a sandy shore. His mouth was dry, and he kept his thumb on the gun hammer, ready to fire.

CHAPTER 2

WHEN HE HAD gone she stood listening, oblivious of the camp sounds and conversation, but she heard nothing. There was no shot, no shout . . . nothing.

He had ridden into the shadow beside the stable and paused there, but when he moved from that shadow into the outer darkness she had no idea.

He was gone.

Irina Carnarvon felt a curious sense of loss . . . a ridiculous thought, for the man was not her sort, anyway. Yet the feeling remained, and she asked herself, What was her sort?

What sort of man did she want? What sort of life? It was an odd question, for she had believed that was settled in her mind. She had thought to marry Frederick, and it was unreasonable that a ride of a few miles with a strange, unshaved, unwashed man of the desert could change that.

Nor had it been changed. Only there was a subtle sort of difference in her feelings now. What had moved her to let him ride Mohammet? She had never allowed Frederick to ride the horse, and actually, aside from one groom on their estate in Wales, nobody had ridden him but her father and herself.

What was her sort? What kind of man did she want? And what sort of man was this man called Shalako?

Certainly, she did not want him. She did not know

him, and then he was only a wanderer, a hunter, big, uncouth . . . but was that fair? What made her say he was
uncouth? Actually, there was a strangely gentle quality
in the man . . . it was in nothing he had said, rather his
handling of his horse, and aside from his brusque way of
speaking, his manner toward her.

Yet it was he who caused her to think of herself and
of Frederick. Not for a long time had she thought as she
was thinking now.

This man had come up from the desert, and now he
had returned to it.

Who was he? What was he?

Above all, who was *she*? She had scarcely known her
mother, living much in a world of men. Her father had
never been content with the hunting of Wales or of Scot-
land. He had hunted wild boar in France as a boy, and
then had gone to Africa. She herself had been to Africa
and to India with him.

Her father held an ancient title, possessed ancient
wealth, but he had been a hunter. Never so much at home
as when he was far from home and in the deep woods, the
far veldt, the desert, the mountains.

———

THE TABLE HAD been set up on a stretch of hard-packed
adobe clay, swept clean of dust. Now it was spread with
white linen, set with silver and glass. It seemed strangely
incongruous in the midst of this desert, yet it had never
seemed so before.

Charles and Edna Dagget were already seated at the
table, with Julia Paige and Laura Davis opposite them.
They looked up as she approached.

"I never knew anyone like her, Julia," Laura said, with

a teasing smile. "She rides out into an empty desert and comes back with a man."

"And what a man! Where is he, Irina? Don't tell me you let him get away?"

"Yes, he's gone."

She looked around with wonderment. All this, these pleasant people at the table, the others that would soon join them, this was her world . . . but what was it doing here? Suddenly, with a kind of embarrassment, she realized how foolish all this must have seemed to Shalako.

Like a group of children they had come running into this country to play, this country where everything was the utmost in reality. For there was something positive about the desert . . . it was stark, strong, definite. There were few shadings here, and many points of no return. The margin between life and death was infinitely narrow.

Pete Wells . . . in the morning she had talked with him, a quiet, rather colorless man, yet a man, filled with life, enjoying his small pleasures. And a few hours later he was dead, shot down by men he had not even seen.

Count Henri came up to the table and joined them. He was a tall, well set-up man with a shading of silver at the temples. He had been a soldier in the French Army, serving somewhere in the Far East, and he had written a book on China, a scholarly work which she had not read.

"I am sorry he went away," he said, "I liked the look of the man, and if there is trouble, he would have been a good man to have around."

Von Hallstatt overheard the comment. "There won't be trouble, Henri. I was just talking with Hockett and he assures me the Apaches are all south of the border or on reservations."

"Mightn't it be a good idea to pull out in the morning, Fred?" Henri watched the food being placed on the table. "I don't like the look of things."

Von Hallstatt glanced at him. "Don't tell me you've got the wind up? Hockett says that the Apaches rarely move in groups larger than twenty or thirty, and no party that small would be likely to attack us. We're too many for them."

He paused. "No, Henri, I came down here to get a desert bighorn, and I shall. And if we have a bit of a skirmish, so much the better."

Henri glanced across the table at von Hallstatt, a cool, measuring glance. "It is not as if we were all men," he said. "I doubt if we have the right to subject the ladies to such risk."

"There is no risk." Von Hallstatt glanced up at him. "Forget it, Henri. This man frightened Irina with some talk of Indians. I have no idea what he hoped to gain. Or perhaps I do. At least he rode away on our finest horse."

"I believed him," Irina said quietly, "and I still believe him."

Von Hallstatt smiled at her. "I am afraid he impressed you too much. Did you not tell me you had read the novels of Fenimore Cooper? I am afraid you see your man from the desert as another Leatherstocking."

Irina smiled. "And he may be. I think we could use one now."

The conversation took a turn away from the moment, but Irina was silent, scarcely hearing the talk that went around and across the table. She was thinking again of the man who had ridden into the night on her favorite horse . . . Would she see him again?

Von Hallstatt talked easily. He was a good conversationalist, if somewhat opinionated, and not quite so easy with words as Count Henri. An inordinately proud man, he was undoubtedly brilliant. Long ago, when she first met him in London, she had been told that had he not gone into the military he might have become a brilliant mathematician.

She looked up, feeling eyes upon her. Across the table and back at the edge of the firelight was the man called Bosky Fulton. He looked at her without smiling, but there was a boldness in his eyes that irritated her. She looked away, taking up a comment of Henri's but her thoughts remained with Fulton.

He made her uneasy . . . there was something unclean about the man that had little to do with his physical dirtiness, something that warned and repelled her. For that matter, aside from Buffalo and that other young man, the one who drove the wagon—Harding, his name was—she found little to like in any of the men Frederick hired.

When they were outfitting none of the men recommended to them had cared to join up. These men were fiercely independent and they resented Frederick's manner. He was accustomed to Germanic subservience to authority, and persisted in regarding the men he hired as servants or peasants, and no one could call these men either. Work for you they might, but they remained themselves, proud, independent, and prepared to fight to preserve their independence.

The result had been that the men he could get were the worst, the scum, the hangers-on. Even Pete Wells had objected to the hiring of Rio Hockett . . . but when Fulton appeared Wells simply turned away and would say nothing. Like the others, Wells had been afraid of Fulton.

She looked down at her plate, appetite suddenly gone. For the first time in days she thought of her father, and wished he was here. He had been a calm, sure man who always seemed to know what to do, and who had an unerring judgment of men.

She looked up. "Frederick, why don't we go back?"

He took his wineglass in his fingers and turned it slowly, watching the reflection of the firelight in the wine.

"We came for a hunt. You knew when we came how long we would be gone, and we had planned this hunt in detail. I do not wish to leave."

"We might do better in the mountains near Silver City," Henri suggested. "There is plenty of timber there."

"You, too, Henri? Don't tell me you are afraid? I thought the French were a bold, dashing lot? Reckless, and all that?"

Henri's eyes chilled, but he smiled. "Dashing? Yes. But cautious also, and lovers of comfort. I believe a move to the north would offer more of both."

"And I do not."

Julia Paige lifted her large, dark eyes and looked down the table at Frederick. Irina felt a little tightening inside, knowing what Julia was going to say. Julia had made no secret of her interest in Frederick.

"After coming all this way it would be foolish to go back emptyhanded. I think we should stay. At least we should stay long enough to see if Irina's desert man will come back again."

"I am perfectly prepared to stay," Charles Dagget said. "We have only just come, and there seems no reason to be frightened. If there are Indians, I have no doubt the Army can cope with them."

"Yes," Irina said as she arose. "I believe they could cope with them . . . if they knew where they were, and where we were." She smiled sweetly. "You will remember, Charles, that the Army has no idea we are here."

She walked away, going toward the stable. She had never been inside the building, but this was the one Shalako had suggested they could defend.

Harding was seated near the door, but when she approached he got quickly to his feet. "Howdy, ma'am. Something I can do for you?"

"Would you show me the stable, Mr. Harding? Mr. Carlin was saying it would make a fort."

"Sure would! I been looking it over, ma'am, and whoever built this knew a thing or two. Old, mighty old, but strong. And the portholes are placed just right to cover everything."

Within the barn Harding held up a lantern. It was a long room, and there had been stalls for eight horses, a storeroom for harness, and a big area where hay had been kept. There was a steep stair that led to the loft.

"There's a bigger room upstairs," Harding explained. "They must have lived there for a time." He led the way up the steps and showed her the room up there.

The floors were solid, the planks well fitted. There were loopholes here also, and, from a large window, Irina could look out over the entire camp, lighted as it was by campfires.

The wagons had been drawn into the gaps between the buildings, but there was no evidence of alertness among the men, to say nothing of those who lingered about the table.

The sky was scattered with stars, the black serrated ridge of the mountains rimmed the sky, and there was a velvety coolness in the night.

"Mr. Harding, have you lived long in the West?"

"Yes, ma'am. Since I was eleven. Before that my home was Ohio. Raised on a farm, ma'am, and done a sight of hunting back there.

"We came West and my family was wiped out by Kiowas while I was from home, visitin'. I've been freighting and buffalo hunting since then. Done a mite of rough carpentering here and there."

"What do you think? Are we in danger of attack?"

"Yes, ma'am. Where there's Apaches there's danger. Or most any Indians, for that matter. War is a way of life to them. They count wealth in horses, and a man who can steal horses better than somebody else is a big man, a mighty big man."

"Mr. Harding, that man . . . Shalako . . . he suggested we think of defending this place if it becomes so bad we cannot defend the circle. He thought we should have food and ammunition here, prepared ahead of time."

"That's good thinking."

"He also suggested that we keep someone we can trust inside here, or close by. I want you to be that man, Mr. Harding."

"Yes, ma'am. Begging your pardon, ma'am, as long as we're on the subject. This is a mighty poor lot of men you have here. I wouldn't place much dependence on them, and that Fulton, ma'am, he's a bad lot, a bad lot."

She turned away from the window and walked to the

steps. At the head of the steps she paused again. "Mr. Harding? What do you know about Shalako?"

Roy Harding was a lean, raw-boned young man, not tall, but muscular and fit. He paused near her. "I never saw him before, but I'd heard tell of him, ma'am. Buffalo, he knew him a long time back. Shalako grew up out here, ma'am. Someplace in California, I think, and then lived in Texas awhile. When he was eighteen or so he pulled out and it was six or eight years before he showed up around again, and then it was up in Montana.

"Nobody knows much about him except that he's said to be one of the best shots on the frontier. He can track better than most Indians, and can ride anything that wears hair.

"Buffalo Harris says he's hell-on-wheels in any kind of a fight." Harding paused. "I sure wish he'd stayed with us."

———

VON HALLSTATT GLANCED around as Irina returned to the table, but offered no comment. A servant was filling their glasses again. "You must try this, Henri. It is one of our finest German wines."

"A good wine, a very good wine."

"Ah? I was not aware that the French ever conceded there was any good wine but French wine."

"On the contrary, Baron, if it has quality, no matter what it is, we French have it. We have learned how to be content with the best of everything."

"There is a story behind this *Bernkasteler Doktor*. It is said there was a certain bishop who had fallen ill of some confusing illness, and no matter what the doctors did for him, he continued to lose strength.

"Finally, or so the story goes, an old soldier who was

a friend of the bishop filled a keg with *Bernkasteler* and, in spite of the protests, wheeled it into the bishop's room and filled a glass with it, and then another.

"The following morning the bishop was much better, and he declared, 'This wine, this fine doctor, has cured me!' Hence, the name of the wine."

"It is growing cold," Edna Dagget said. "I believe I will go in."

Charles arose and walked with her toward the wagon where they slept.

"She is not fitted for this life," von Hallstatt said. "Charles would have done well to leave her behind."

Irina glanced at him, and said, "Wives are not so easily left behind. A wife's place is with her husband."

"Not at war," von Hallstatt replied, "nor the hunt. Still, hers was a good idea. It grows late and tomorrow I want to try for a bighorn." He got to his feet. "Good night, my friends."

He turned from the table and walked away, and for a moment there was silence. Then Count Henri said, "And how about you, Julia? Are you going with us tomorrow?"

Julia Paige smiled quickly. "Of course, I cannot leave all the hunting to Irina."

Laura Davis had been quiet. "You know," she said, "I agree with you, Henri, and with Irina. I think we should leave, as quickly as possible."

When Julia started to object, she continued. "My father entertained General Crook one evening while I was at home, and they discussed the Apache. Some of the stories were horrible, utterly horrible! They did not know I was listening," she added.

Hans Kreuger shrugged. "I trust the baron," he said. "He is a man of great judgment and discretion."

"It is different here," Laura said. "I think we should go."

"You heard what he said," Irina replied, "and we are his guests."

Count Henri slowly filled his pipe. "I think we should go, Hans. There is no game here that we cannot find farther north, and under pleasanter circumstances."

"Except Apaches." Hans glanced over at Henri. "I know the baron seriously wishes for a bit of fighting. I have heard him express his contempt for this American Army that chases Indians but cannot catch them."

"Has he had experience with guerrilla warfare, Hans?" Henri asked gently. "I have . . . much like this, I think, for I fought in the mountains and desert against the Arabs in North Africa.

"Luckily, I had read Washington's comments on Braddock's defeat by Indians and was cautious. Believe me, the circumstances are much different, and no tactics so far taught in Europe can prepare an army for that kind of fighting."

"Speaking of tactics," Kreuger commented, "I wonder what school the man Shalako attended?"

"School?" Henri glanced around at the young German. "I understood he had lived here all his life."

"Perhaps . . . but he mentioned Jomini, Saxe, and Vegetius. I should not expect to hear them mentioned by a buffalo hunter, or whatever he is."

Henri walked off toward her wagon with Julia, and Hans followed. There was a slight stir of wind that ruffled the flames. Buffalo came from the shadows and added fuel to the fire, yet he did not build the big flames.

The bed of coals glowed a deep red, here and there a

yellow tendril of flame lifting with the smoke toward the stars.

"You liked him, didn't you?" Laura said.

"Him?" Irina looked up, startled. Then she laughed, knowing evasion was impossible and slightly ridiculous. "I don't know. I never knew anyone quite like him."

"Except your father."

"Oh . . . not very much. They both like wild country. I don't think that makes any difference, anyway."

"And both of them are those big, self-contained men who do everything well. And Shalako is a handsome man, Irina."

"I never really looked at him . . . not that way. Somehow it did not seem to matter. It was something else that impressed me. I cannot remember ever feeling so safe as I was with him."

There was silence between them, and she looked out over the desert, wondering. Where was he now? Was he still riding? Westward, perhaps?

"It's very silly," she said suddenly, "talking this way about, well, a man like that. There's no telling what he really is, and, after all, a girl just doesn't go running off with any man who rides in out of the desert."

Irina remained watching the stars over the mountains long after Laura had gone to bed. The general, Baron Frederick von Hallstatt, was a man of strength and courage, an interesting man in every sense, but hard in a way that she did not like. Occasionally, and rarely to be sure, he had shown an utter disregard for the feelings of others, even including herself, that was disturbing.

He was ruthless, that she accepted. So for that matter was this stranger, this man Shalako who had suddenly occupied so much of their thinking by merely appearing on the scene. Shalako was ruthless, she knew this at once, but his ruthlessness would be applied to enemies, not to those close to him.

A lonely man, traveling alone and living alone, he was nevertheless far from selfish. That he had ridden off into the desert to leave them was, seeing it as he did, simply good sense.

Their party had not been invited into this area, and what had begun as a sort of lark when the excitement of hunting buffalo had palled, had suddenly turned into something foolhardy and dangerous.

When she had first accepted the baron's invitation to hunt on the prairies and in the mountains it had seemed tremendously exciting. Many Europeans had come west to hunt on the plains. Hunters talked as much of hunting buffalo in America as they talked of hunting lions in Africa or tigers in India.

The element of danger from possibly hostile tribes added spice to the idea, and yet seemed very remote. It was one thing to talk of hostile Indians in the fashionable restaurants of New York or Saratoga, and quite another thing to face the danger of attack in a remote desert.

What had seemed exciting in a conversation at Delmonico's in New York was frightful here, and she was not calmed by Frederick von Hallstatt's attitude.

The fact remained that Pete Wells was dead, and his death was in part her own fault.

In part it was all their faults for coming out here in the first place. How many more would die before this venture ended? If there was no attack, they should leave. Suddenly, she resolved. Regardless of what the others did, she was going to Fort Cummings as Shalako had advised and then back home.

The crunch of a boot on the gravel behind her was her only warning. And then the smell of stale, unwashed clothing before the voice spoke.

"Waitin' for somebody, ma'am?" It was Bosky Fulton. "If you are, you just don't have to wait no longer."

She turned and measured him coolly. "I am waiting for no one. Will you step aside?"

Fulton made no effort to move. "You're goin' to need a friend, so don't come it so high and mighty over me, ma'am. You better make up your mind that you're goin' to be nice to me, or else you'll find yourself in the hands of some Apache . . . and that could be worse. Could be." He chuckled.

"Will you step aside?"

Fulton hesitated, grinning insultingly, and then he stepped aside and as she walked toward her wagon, he said, "And if you want to get that general of yours killed, you just tell him what I said."

She was trembling when she reached the wagon and she stopped, her knees shaking. She remembered then some of the talk around the camp, that Bosky Fulton was a gunman who had killed several men in gun battles.

Suddenly there was no safety anywhere, and the night seemed filled with crowding menace.

She started to get into the wagon, then hesitated again. Would they not be safer in the upper room at the stable? If she and Laura, and some of the others . . . ?

SHALAKO HEARD THE whisper of the approaching riders coming through the sand, and he eased his position in the saddle, holding the Colt ready to fire.

The horsemen, riding single file, came like ghosts out

of the night, and for an instant each Indian was starkly outlined against the sky as he reached the edge of the wash, then dipping into it he dipped into shadow and was gone, like the targets in a shooting gallery. There were six.

Only those brief, momentary shadows, a whisper of hoofs in the sand, the rattle of a stone as they left the wash, and they were gone.

He walked the Arab steadily into the night, holding his pace down, wanting no Apache to smell dust as he had smelled it, for others might be coming.

There was a canyon of which he knew, a canyon that reached back into the mountains south of Gillespie Peak, and there was a place there he might hole up. Farther up the canyon there was a trickle of water that occasionally flowed in the early months of the year.

He walked the stallion for approximately three miles, then touched him lightly with a spur and let the Arab run. The horse ran tirelessly until the black wall of the mountain loomed over them. He knew when he had reached the mouth of the canyon by the sudden coolness of the air, and turned the Arab.

Twice he rode past the place he sought, but finally he located the small hollow, shielded from the rest of the canyon by brush and boulders. There was an acre or so of sparse grass where water from the spring kept it fresh. There he unsaddled and picketed the horse on the grass.

Spreading his groundsheet and blankets, he stretched out with a sigh, easing his tired muscles and closing his lids over eyes that ached from the strain of watching a far land under a blazing sun. Once more he opened his eyes to look up at the pinnacle of the mountain, and the last sound he heard was the placid munching of the horse, close beside him.

LIEUTENANT COLONEL GEORGE A. Forsyth, in command at Fort Cummings, replaced the letter on his desk and was for a moment swept by a wave of helpless fury. His lips tightened and he sat very still, fighting down his anger before he looked up at Lieutenant McDonald.

The colonel pushed the letter across his desk. "Look at this! Of all the damned fools!"

McDonald took the letter and read it through twice before realizing all it implied.

> *Fort Concho, Texas*
> *April 3, 1882*
>
> *Officer Commanding,*
> *Fort Cummings,*
> *New Mexico Territory*
>
> *Sir:*
> *   The Baron (General) Frederick von Hallstatt*
> *and party, believed in your area. Last seen,*
> *vicinity of Lost Horse Lake, buffalo hunting.*
> *Eight wagons, twenty-odd persons, including four*
> *white women. One of the latter is Lady Irina*
> *Carnarvon, another is the daughter of U.S.*
> *Senator Y. F. Davis. Locate, and escort out of the*
> *area.*
>
> *Sincerely,*
> *John A. Russell,*
> *General Commanding*

Lieutenant McDonald was shocked. "My God! Four *women*! At a time like this!"

Colonel Forsyth tapped his pencil on the edge of the desk and studied the map before him. If von Hallstatt's party had been in the vicinity of Lost Horse Lake on or before the third it was just possible they had reached this area. But why would they come *here*?

Antelope were the only game, and there were more of those in the country from which they had just come. In the mountains there were bighorn sheep, but they also could be found farther north. The desert mountains to the south were bleak and inhospitable to an outsider, offering little, promising less.

A veteran Indian fighter, dangerously wounded in the Beecher Island fight in which Roman Nose was killed, he respected the Indian as a fighting man, and knew few warriors more cunning than Chato existed.

The barrel-chested, flat-nosed Apache had the torso of a two-hundred-pound man on his stocky body, and enough battle lust for a dozen men of his size. Not an hour before had come word that Chato was over the border and moving north.

Moreover, Nachita and Loco had fled the San Carlos reservation with a party of young braves who were spoiling for a fight, and undoubtedly the two groups would meet somewhere to the south. And right in the middle of the country where the meeting was likely to take place was a party of casual tourists, ignorant of the desert and the Apache. If anything happened to any one of them he would be replying by endorsement to the War Department for the next two years.

Colonel Forsyth's force was too small and the area he was expected to patrol too large. Military forces much larger than his had failed to pin down the will-o'-the-wisp of an Apache band. Chato would be sure to raid north and east, trying meanwhile to augment his forces still further by drawing upon discontented elements at San Carlos.

For months Forsyth's scouts at the reservation had warned that trouble was stirring.

"Lieutenant," Forsyth said at last, "I want you to take your scouts and ride west toward Stein's Peak, then swing back a little south of east and come up toward the Hatchets. If you cut the trail of those wagons go in and bring them out of there. Understand?"

"Yes, sir . . . I have heard, sir, that von Hallstatt can be difficult."

"You are a soldier, McDonald. Bring him out of there."

"Yes, sir."

"Lieutenant Hall will make a scout toward the Hatchets, so be on the lookout for him. I shall follow with six troops of the Fourth Cavalry."

When McDonald had gone, Sandy Forsyth sat back in his chair and considered the situation. He was a handsome, square-jawed man with the scars of his wounds to prove what Indians could do. Trust an Indian to know of any movement in the area . . . there was not the slightest possibility that Chato did not know of the von Hallstatt group.

Hall would swing south and west, McDonald south and east, so if von Hallstatt was in the area they would be sure to cut his trail. At the same time their pincers movement might catch Chato in between. Meanwhile he would come down from the north with the Fourth Cavalry.

The colonel scowled as he studied the map. That was

the way he had planned it and that was how it was supposed to work. The difficulty was that things almost never worked as planned, for Chato and his band would break up and proceed as individual members to a predetermined rendezvous. He had seen such groups fragment before, leaving nothing but a confusion of tracks almost impossible to follow.

Von Hallstatt had horses, and by the time the Apaches came up with his party, the Apache would need horses.

So few men, so much territory. Forsyth walked to the window and looked out. Somewhere in all that dusty, brown vastness was a party of dusty, brown bodies, bodies with hard faces and narrow eyes, scanning the desert as he was scanning it. And those bodies were those of forty or fifty of the most dangerous fighting men on earth.

The moves had been made, and it remained to see what happened. His task was to reach von Hallstatt before the Apaches did and, if possible, to capture or defeat the Apaches.

He swore bitterly. A party of casual hunters had gone in boldly, carelessly, where companies of soldiers rode with caution.

———

LYING ON HER pallet in the upper room at the stable, Irina could not sleep. It had taken all her arguments and persuasive powers to convince the others that they should move from their comfortable beds in the wagons to the stable, but even now she was not satisfied.

Only Laura Davis had listened and agreed, but Laura's mind had been made up beforehand. Edna Dagget had complained of the trouble, Julia Paige had scoffed mildly, but with a bit of a bite to her scoffing, too.

Julia had long had her cap set for Baron von Hallstatt, a fact of which only von Hallstatt seemed unaware, and it irked Julia to see Irina walking off so easily with the man she wanted.

Lying in the darkness, Irina stared up at the ceiling overhead, and considered the people with whom she faced this emergency, if such it would prove to be.

With the exception of Count Henri, none of these people had ever faced any kind of a difficulty, or were less prepared to deal with an emergency.

Frederick had been a highly successful officer in a highly organized army, accustomed to issuing orders and seeing them obeyed, yet the organization of that army was such that it left little initiative to any of its officers.

He had won victories over a disorganized, retreating foe, one whose generals had grown old and tired in their positions and who thought in terms of wars long completed and over. Frederick had received orders and given them, but there had been little chance for improvisation.

How would he react against an enemy when he would receive no orders himself, and where he must fight in person against an elusive enemy?

Count Henri, somewhat older than Frederick, was in many ways much younger. Henri had fought against Frederick in the Franco-Prussian War, but what was more important, Henri had served in the African desert against a foe much like the present one. Yet he was a man who talked little.

Frederick was brave . . . of that she had no doubt, yet more and more she was beginning to be aware that he was not only terribly self-centered, but that he was also without imagination.

Charles Dagget was not a fighting man. He was a diplomat, shrewd enough, congenial, and pleasant company always. This was his first venture into any wilderness greater than the environs of Paris or London. Furthermore, he was not suited to a rugged life.

Edna Dagget was a pretty woman, too thin, and apt to become somewhat hysterical . . . yet a lovely and gracious person under normal circumstances.

Laura Davis was the only American among them, a pleasant, charming girl, just short of being really beautiful, and a fine horsewoman. She had traveled in Europe, lived in Washington and New York, and had hunted in Virginia and Kentucky.

Hans Kreuger had been Frederick's aide during a brief period at the Franco-Prussian War's end. A serious, capable young man from a poor but honorable family. Like Frederick and Henri, he was an excellent rifle shot.

Edna loathed guns, and Charles had never fired any kind of a gun until this trip, and was notably poor as a rifle shot. Julia was an excellent horsewoman but uninterested in guns . . . as for herself, she had hunted with her father from childhood, killing her first wild boar at fourteen with her father standing by, and her first lion at seventeen.

Hours after she finally dropped off to sleep she awakened with a start, staring wide-eyed at the roof above. For a moment she could not recall where she was. The faint glow from the dying fire reflected on the underside of the roof, coming through the wide open door at the side of the building, which they had opened to get fresh air.

Otherwise, it was quite dark and she could hear no sound from the outside. Careful to make no sound so as not to disturb the others, she got to her feet and tiptoed to the door.

The fire was a bed of glowing red coals with only a few tendrils of flame doing their weird ballet above them. Beside the fire, his chin on his chest and evidently asleep, was the sentry.

The area within the circle of buildings was perhaps thirty yards long by twenty wide, and the firelight flickered on the canvas wagon tops and made weird, dancing shadows around their spokes. A few men slept under the wagons.

Nothing stirred in the space below, yet she stood for an instant, enjoying the stillness of the night and the red glow of the coals. Then from the corner of her eye she seemed to detect movement near the fire.

The guard was slumped forward, the black log near the fire was . . . *there had been no log*!

She reached quickly for her rifle, but even as her hand grasped it, the log came suddenly erect, a knife flashed in the firelight, and the guard toppled forward, falling at the edge of the fire.

She fired . . . too quickly. The Indian turned as if stunned and looked up at her. She saw the wide, hard-boned face and the dark holes where deep-sunk eyes would be, and then a second shot merged with the echo of her own. The Indian took two staggering steps and fell on his face.

From outside the circle there was a sudden chorus of yells and then a rush of hoofs that turned into a thunder of racing horses and mules . . . and then the sound died and there was only the dead guard and the naked dusty, brown figure sprawled face down on the hardpacked earth to indicate that anything had happened.

Men came from all over the yard, rushing out, then ducking for cover as there was an outburst of firing. She had never seen men take cover so quickly.

Edna Dagget sat up, clutching the blankets to her breast. "What is it? What has happened?"

"We've been attacked." Irina was surprised at her own calm. "A man has been killed."

Irina dressed quickly, and beside her Laura was dressing also. Irina took up her rifle and started toward the steps. Edna Dagget stared at her, frightened. "Where are you going? Why is everybody dressing? It isn't even daylight."

"We should all dress and be ready to help. A man has been killed."

"*Killed?*" Edna Dagget's shrill cry faded into a gasp of horror, and she started to dress also.

For the moment there was no further shooting. After the outburst of sound the silence was frightening. Stars held still in the sky, and the night was velvet soft. It was unreasonable that a man was dead . . . two men.

She went to the guard and, taking his sleeve, pulled him away from the edge of the fire that was already smoldering in his coat.

Buffalo called softly. "Ma'am! Get out of the light! *Quick!*"

She turned quickly and sprang away from the fire just as a bullet kicked sparks near where she had been standing.

She knelt beside Buffalo, at the rear wheel of a wagon. There was something reassuring about his stalwart body.

He was unshaved, and probably unbathed, but he possessed an air of competence that gave her confidence.

Buffalo had drawn up the old chopping block and a couple of loose rocks for added protection.

"If I had been a moment sooner I could have saved that guard. I did not recognize that Indian until just before he moved."

"Figured that was you shooting. You set him right up for me. That was good thinking, ma'am."

Inordinately pleased at the compliment, she crouched lower, looking out into the darkness. Here and there she could make out clumps of creosote bush, but nothing more.

For the first time she thought of what had happened and its meaning to them. The Apaches had stampeded their wagon stock and now they were immobilized unless they wished to abandon all their belongings. The saddle stock had all been held inside the circle . . . a small concession to Shalako's warning.

"Were there no guards outside the circle?"

"Two. Look close and you can see one of them lying out there. He's the lucky one, he's dead."

Vague recollections returned to mind of stories she had heard, and only half-listened to, about what Indians did to prisoners. Suddenly the night was filled with menace, and with horror.

The castle in Wales where she had lived, London, Paris, New York . . . they seemed to be in another world.

"How much chance do we have?"

With other women he might have lied, but he respected the coolness and intelligence of this girl and she seemed somehow one of them. In part it was her own attitude and quickness with the rifle, in part it was the fact that she had loaned a horse to Shalako.

"Less'n fifty-fifty, I'd say. Ma'am, I ain't a-lyin' to you, you keep one bullet for yourself, d' you hear?"

She had never thought of death as something that could happen to her . . . older people died, or lives were lost in accidents, and she heard of them or read of them in newspapers and was rarely stirred. The facility with which people bore the hardships of others was amazing.

She had always known that someday she would die. We are born with this knowledge or acquire it soon after birth, but death always seems remote and far-off. To realize there was no special protection for her . . . that she, Lady Irina Carnarvon, could die a bloody and cruel death out here in these sand hills filled her with horror and distaste.

"He was right to leave us," she said.

"Mighty independent man. Wish he was here, though."

Buffalo Harris was doing some thinking of his own. How did a man get himself into a fix like this? How long had he been learning about Indians, anyway? Since he was six, crouched in a cornfield with his sister, listening to the awful, dying screams of his father and mother. He had fought Sioux, Kiowa, and Comanche, and certainly knew better than to latch onto a greenhorn outfit like this.

It didn't make any kind of sense, the things a man would do. He was loafing around and not even broke when the offer came, and the others were taking it up, so he did, too. It sounded like a few months of mighty easy living and good grub . . . now he would be lucky to get out with his hair.

"Have you known him long?"

Buffalo shifted the tobacco to his other cheek. Odd, how good tobacco tasted when time was a-wasting.

"Awhile. He's a man minds his own affairs, and doesn't wait around much. I mean he rides in and if something isn't taking on to interest him, first thing you know, he's gone.

"He prospects a mite, rides herd once in a while. Been over the trail to Kansas with cowherds a couple of times, and one way or another, he keeps busy."

With faint gray where night's darkness had been, the Apaches came out of the desert like ghosts, running silently in a staggered skirmish line. Buffalo, whose eyes had never stopped searching, nailed the first one off the ground.

He saw the warrior's knee buckle at his shot, and then the girl beside him was shooting, and she put a bullet into the chest of the man he had wounded. And then they vanished like puffs of smoke . . . only they were closer now.

Buffalo turned his shaggy head to grin at her. "Two for us. Ma'am, you must have done a sight of shootin'."

Von Hallstatt ran up and dropped to the earth beside them. His eyes were hot with excitement. "They move quickly." He pointed with the muzzle of his rifle. "One dropped to the ground out there, and when he rises, I shall kill him."

"He shifted position soon as he hit dirt," Buffalo advised. "They always do."

Von Hallstatt glanced at him irritably, then turned his eyes back to the desert. The light was growing now . . . he would not have believed that thirty or forty men lay within rifle shot.

As if speaking only to Irina, Buffalo began to discuss the Apache. "Start figurin' 'em like other folks an' you'll get yourself killed. You never get more than a split-second shot at an Apache, and in a setup like this they attack on foot, all scattered out. An' they can wait . . . time means nothin' to an Indian."

"Why don't they attack?" von Hallstatt demanded impatiently.

"Eatin' your wagon stock, most likely. They don't figure we'll be goin' anyplace."

Irina felt a chill of apprehension. Lying on the cold ground, her eyes searched the desert, but she saw nothing.

She heard movement behind them and glanced around to see a teamster hurrying toward the tank with a bucket. Yet even as she looked he seemed to stumble, his knees crumpled and the sound of a shot battered against the hills as he toppled face downward upon the sand.

Von Hallstatt's rifle had come up sharply, expectantly, but there was nothing at which to shoot, simply nothing at all.

"Three men killed, one missing," Buffalo spat into the sand, "an' we killed maybe two of them."

The hours dragged. Irina slipped from her position and careful to keep under cover, returned to the stable.

Laura had a fire going and coffee on. Mako was breaking eggs into a frying pan. Over at the house where most of the teamsters had slept, another fire was going. There was an occasional shot.

Charles Dagget was breaking down the partition between two stalls for fuel, and making an awkward job of it.

It was early, but already the sun was hot.

Suddenly, the morning air was rent by a shocking scream of pure agony, the scream of an animal in mortal anguish. Irina came up, her eyes wide with horror, and Edna clapped both hands over her ears. It came again, that same hoarse, choking scream . . . the scream of something in pain beyond belief.

Von Hallstatt cried out, "What in God's name is *that*?"

"Now"—Buffalo rolled his tobacco in his cheek and spat—"now we know where that other horse guard is."

THE SOUND OF gunfire awakened him. He lay on his back staring up at the last of the stars, listening.

He picked up the cigarette he had carefully rolled the night before and put it between his lips. As he struck his match, there were other shots. At least they had not been caught sleeping. They would make a fight of it then.

His mouth tasted bad and the stubble on his jaw itched. He should have been twenty miles along the Tucson trail.

He threw off his blanket and sat up, careful to check the cliffs around with cool, dispassionate eyes. He was a man without illusions, and there was no reason to believe that all the Apaches were over yonder at the point of the Hatchets. He might have picked up a few himself.

The Arab nickered softly and came up to be petted and scratched, making a show of pulling away from his hand, but not doing it.

He saddled the horse first, ready to ride out in a hurry

if need be. Then he took up his rifle and led the horse to the trickle of water. His rifle would not change what was happening back there, and he saw no reason to get himself killed because of another man's mistakes. He made enough mistakes of his own without paying for another man's.

Nor was he opposed to boy generals. The younger ones were the best, as time and history had proved again and again. Napoleon had completed his Italian campaign by the time he was twenty-five, Hannibal was thirty-three at the Battle of Cannae, Alexander the Great had been twenty-five at the Battle of Arbela, and Wolfe had been thirty-two at the Battle of Quebec . . . he could think of fifty others.

The older ones were slower to change their ways, always wishing to fight new battles the way they had won old ones.

From time to time there were solitary shots . . . more than likely fired by the defenders who probably were seeing Indians where there were none.

He broke some branches from an antelope bush and fed them to the Arab. The stallion nosed doubtfully at the strange stuff, curling his lips around the leaves, hesitant, but aware that for some reason the man wanted him to eat them. Trying them, he liked the taste, and accepted more.

"You'd better learn, boy. You won't have oats very often, traveling with me."

He left his night camp then, and concealed the horse high up in the rocks where there was more antelope bush and another forage plant called wool fat. Then seated against the rock that offered the best position, he studied the situation.

The problem was not one to be solved by a lot of dashing about and shooting. If solved at all it would be by thinking, thinking first and carefully.

It was reasonable to suppose that only a small part of the Apaches were involved at the ranch. As the smoke signals told him, Chato was seeking reinforcements from San Carlos, and some of the Indians had left the reservation to join him.

Moreover, owing to the necessity of living off the country, the Apaches coming up from Mexico were traveling in more than one group, hence one could never be sure of where to expect an enemy.

Colonel Forsyth was in command at Fort Cummings, and would be out in force to round up the Indians.

If some trick could draw off the attackers at the ranch, then the group there might be gotten away to Fort Cummings or into a better defensive position in the mountains. At the ranch, the defenders would be driven to the buildings eventually, and cut off from water.

Putting himself in Forsyth's position, Shalako tried to guess the moves that would be made. Both the Animas and Playas valleys offered highroads into Mexico for the fleeing Apaches. Hence troops would surely be sent south along the Hatchets and along the Pelonchillos.

As always at these heights in the southwestern deserts, the air was unbelievably clear. From where he sat the ranch buildings were quite visible, as were the white tops of the wagons. He could distinguish no features of either, but the place itself was clear and sharp.

What was the old rule for judging distance? At one mile the trunks of large trees could be distinguished, at something over two miles—say two miles and a half—one could distinguish chimneys and windows, at six miles windmills and towers could be seen, and at nine miles a church steeple could be recognized.

The rules were for average atmosphere, much thicker than the clear desert air. In the desert there was no smoke, dust, or moisture as a rule, and only one-fourth the atmosphere of the eastern states, consequently one could see much farther.

Seated on a rock in the morning sun, Shalako watched the ranch and considered the problem in all its aspects. There was just a chance that a smoke signal might work, and he was going to try.

Heat waves shimmered above a desert where nothing moved. Lying on his stomach at one corner of the ranch house, Frederick von Hallstatt, baron and general, tasted the flavor of bitterness.

Sweat trickled down his forehead and into his eyes. From time to time he dried his palms on his shirt, and licked the sweat from his upper lip with his tongue. Heat waves shimmered, and he squinted into the unreality of the desert with a knot of cold fear clutching at his belly.

On his left, some forty yards away, lay an Apache warrior, one arm thrown wide. To von Hallstatt's knowledge this was the only Indian he had killed and he had fired at least thirty rounds.

He swore bitterly, in German. This was not the kind of fighting he was used to, nor the kind he expected. He glanced around at the others.

Henri faced south from the stable. Buffalo Harris, his skull wrapped in a bloody bandage, was facing west. On the north Charles Dagget held a rifle in unfamiliar hands, and beside him was Roy Harding, late of Ohio, and Bosky Fulton, that ill-smelling, hatchet-faced gunman. Rio Hockett was inside the house.

Early that morning one of the mule skinners had slipped a hand through a wagon flap and stolen a bottle of cognac, and when he stole that bottle he stole death.

The bottle lay out there now, only a third empty, reflecting the morning sun in a bright arrow of light. It had taken only a couple of swallows to make the mule skinner careless, and bottle in hand he started across the open ground toward the stable. The bullet had gone in over his ear, mushroomed, and tore away half his skull when it emerged on the other side.

Inside the stable in the coolest spot on the ground floor lay Hans Kreuger. A handsome young man who danced well in the ballrooms of Berlin, Vienna, and Innsbruck, he lay dying on a pallet against the wall. He had made up his mind to die well, for it was the last thing left to a man, and he had a pride in such matters.

He was a sincere young man who had tried all his life to do things with dignity and manner. He was a proud, but not a vain man, convinced there were certain ways in which a man should conduct himself, and he had lived according to his principles.

It was incredible to him, as it was to von Hallstatt, that their losses had been greater than the attacker's, for it went against all military reason.

Hans Kreuger lay on his back staring up at the ceiling. Whenever anyone on the upper floor of the barn took a step a little puff of dust came through the cracks. Cobwebs trailed their gray nets to catch stray sunbeams . . . perspiration beaded his face but he held himself tight against the pain that was in him and thought of how little a man knows of what destiny has in store.

How proud he had been when he became aide to General von Hallstatt! How proud his parents had been when he was asked to accompany the general on his hunting trip to America, partly as aide to the general, and partly as a guest.

The others of the party would be people a young man of poor family rarely met. It would be a unique opportunity. He had no idea when accepting the offer that he was accepting an invitation to die.

To remain a man and a gentleman to the end, this was all that remained.

Removed from active combat by the bullets that ripped into his body, he could still observe. Laura Davis had grown somehow. She was no longer the friendly, pretty girl, although she was that, also. She was more quiet, more sure of herself. She worked at whatever she did with quick but capable hands. Laura Davis . . . young, beautiful, and exciting. And he lay dying.

Edna Dagget he had once thought frail but lovely, now she was frail and haggard, her loveliness scarcely a memory. Her lips worked with wordless movement, and at every shot, she cringed. A few days ago he had admired her rather biting wit, and her coolness, yet when the emergency developed she proved a hollow shell with nothing inside.

Her husband, whom Edna had always spoken of in disparaging terms, had shown surprising strength. He almost seemed to welcome the fighting. He was entirely ignorant of warfare, yet he was observant, quick to learn, and careful to take no chances.

Hans Kreuger closed his eyes against the ache and the tiredness and tried to remember how the apple trees had looked when they bloomed across the countryside around his home in Hofheim, near Frankfurt. He felt Laura wipe the perspiration from his face, and he opened his eyes to look up at her, proud that he could conceal his pain.

How excited his family had been when he became aide to the baron! He was a powerful man of ancient family and much influence, and Hans's family assured him his fortune was made. How little had any of them known!

How can a man know? How can he guess which decision it is, often an inconsequential one, that sets him irrevocably upon the highway to failure, success, or sudden death? How can a man guess that from one particular instant he is committed, where the cogs will fit, one into the other, and each one turning the wheel inevitably closer and closer? How can he know as he laughs over a glass of wine, as he marches proudly, as he talks softly to a girl on the terrace . . . How can he know that each is a move that brings him closer to the end?

And had he taken another turn, met another girl, drunk his wine in another café, he might have lived a decade longer . . . or three decades even?

In the loft over the stable, Irina yielded her place at the window to Bosky Fulton.

She had been looking out over the desert when she heard faint movement behind her and smelled the stale odor of unwashed clothing. She turned and he leered at her, his shirt collar edged with grime, the grime showing in the skin of his neck.

He grasped her arm and pulled her toward him and she jerked free, astonished and angry.

"Aw, don't look at me that way! Before this is over you'll be glad to ride out of here with somebody who can take care of you."

"I can take care of myself."

"Can you now?" He gestured toward the ladder. "Go ahead an' fix the grub. Meanwhile you better think on this: you cotton up to me or you stay here as bait for those 'Paches. I can get you out of this, and that fancy Fritz Baron of yours, he can't get himself out."

She was trembling with shock and anger when she came down the steps. Yet she was frightened, too, deeply, seriously frightened. And she could not remember being frightened in the same way before this.

One by one the men came for their food, crawling around the rim of the circle, keeping to the small shadow and what protection the buildings and wagons offered.

There was little talk. The men ate quickly, seriously, then returned the way they had come. Only Charles Dagget was excited. "I think I hit one," he said. "Scared him, anyway."

Irina scarcely heard what he said. Should she say anything about what Fulton had told her? And did he really believe what he said? Or was that merely something to use as an argument to her?

He believed it. She suddenly knew that he believed it. Bosky Fulton did not think they were going to get out alive.

Coming after what Shalako had said, she was convinced of their situation. Yet it had not been that which frightened her, but Fulton's own attitude. His cocksureness, his disregard of what would happen to the others, and the sudden sharp awareness that nobody here could protect her. Von Hallstatt was a man of undoubted courage, so was Count Henri, but she had heard enough talk around camp to know that something else was demanded, and she had seen some very tough men walk softly around Bosky Fulton.

Buffalo Harris came in while von Hallstatt and Count Henri were still there. "Smoke over the Animas," Buffalo said. "Wished I knew what they meant. Shalako now, he could read them. He—"

Buffalo broke off sharply, the idea startling him with its possibilities. "No . . . couldn't be that."

"What?"

"By this time he's clean t'other side of the Stein's Peak range, but I was just thinkin', Shalako knowin' the smokes, and all . . . if he sent up a smoke . . . no, it ain't reasonable. Only he savvies that smoke talk as well as any Indian."

"You mean he might send up a signal that would draw them off? But they would come back."

Bosky Fulton descended the ladder. "How's for some coffee?" He grinned insolently at Irina, then glanced at von Hallstatt as if to challenge a reprimand.

"You've left your post." Von Hallstatt eyed him coldly. "Get back up there until you're relieved."

"You want somebody up there," Fulton replied, "you go yourself."

Never had Irina seen such a shocked expression on any man's face as crossed the baron's at that moment. He probably never had had an order refused before.

An instant only . . . then his face was swept by cold fury. His rifle stood near the door. He started for it.

Bosky Fulton's gun slid into his hand, and the cocking of the gun was loud in the sudden silence.

"You pick that up," Fulton drawled, "an' you better walk right outside with it. You turn on me, I'll kill you."

Von Hallstatt stopped. Always before the might of the Prussian Army had stood behind him. Now there was only himself. Never had he been threatened with a pistol, and terrible fury choked him. Yet at the same instant there swept through him the icy realization that he could die. That the man behind him would surely kill.

The baron had been given a choice. Could he lift the rifle, turn and cock and fire before the man behind him could fire?

"Put up your gun, Fulton!" The voice rang with the harshness of command. "Put up your gun and get back to your post."

Of them all, von Hallstatt was the most surprised, for Hans Kreuger had lifted himself to one elbow and in his hands he held the twin barrels of a shotgun, the muzzles pointed at Fulton.

The distance was scarcely twenty feet, the shotgun a short-barreled express gun. Kreuger's face was pale and perspiring, but there was no doubt that he meant what he said.

"I have enough buckshot to cut you in two, Fulton," Kreuger said, "and nothing to lose."

The gunman's eyes seemed to change color. Or was it the light in the room? Irina, who was watching him, saw an ugly hatred come into those yellow eyes, but he eased the hammer back in place with elaborate care, and then he turned and started for the ladder. There he hesitated, stealing a glance over his shoulder, but the twin muzzles followed him relentlessly.

When Fulton had disappeared up the ladder, Kreuger lay back on his pallet, gasping hoarsely, his brow beaded with sweat.

Von Hallstatt remained standing by the door, staring out across the desert, his back to the room. The sun was going down. The day would soon be gone.

He stared blindly, conscious of it all but seeing nothing. He had been afraid. He, Frederick von Hallstatt, had been afraid.

He had known that surely as he stood there that unwashed hireling would kill him. No command of his mattered here, no authority of position or personality stood between him and these men.

He hated them, he hated the wild, irresponsible freedom and independence there was in them all. He was used to subservience, to acceptance of his authority, his position. That independence was in Shalako, Harris, Fulton . . . all of them.

Buffalo Harris's frank, matter-of-fact, man-to-man talk had always offended him, yet it had taken a cocked gun in the hand of Bosky Fulton to make him aware of how little he mattered here. He, Frederick von Hallstatt, baron and general, could be shot down and killed as simply as any peasant.

Turning slowly, he threw a glance at his wounded aide. "Thank you, Hans," he said.

Taking up his rifle he went outside and returned to his position, and not until he was there, watching the desert once more, did he realize that for the first time he had called Kreuger by his given name.

And well he might, for Hans Kreuger had saved him

from more than he knew. Possibly he had saved him from death, possibly from an exhibition of cowardice.

Had Kreuger not intervened, what would he have done? Would he have attempted to turn? Or would he meekly have submitted?

Blindly, Frederick von Hallstatt stared out across the desert. For the first time in his entire life he did not know. For the first time, he was unsure.

CHAPTER 3

W HEN VON HALLSTATT had gone, nobody spoke for several minutes, then Buffalo Harris finished his coffee, and went to the door. He hesitated there, turned as if to speak, then ducked outside and was gone.

Count Henri's handsome features were expressionless. He glanced at her. "I am sorry you are here, Irina."

Then he went outside also.

Her decision, when it was made, was deliberate. And in the moment of deciding she knew it was a decision that should have been made before this. Gathering her skirts, she started for the door.

"Irina!" Laura caught at her arm. "Stay away from the door! What can you be thinking of?"

"I am going to the wagon," she said calmly, "for some food and ammunition."

"You will be killed!"

"I do not think so," she replied calmly, "I think they will want the women alive."

Laura's eyes were without expression. "Yes, yes, of course. But be careful."

It was a silly thing to say at such a time, but what could be said? She took a deep breath and, stepping outside, she walked coolly and deliberately to the nearest wagon.

Climbing into the wagon, she gathered up a parcel of food, a medicine kit with additional medicines, and a box of ammunition. Putting them all in a burlap sack, she swung it over her shoulder and walked back to the stable.

Returning, she climbed into the wagon again. The heat was stifling under the canvas wagon top and the interior smelled of the sun-hot canvas, a smell like no other, yet not unpleasant.

From a box of her own things she took a .44-caliber derringer with two barrels, one over the other. Checking to be sure it was loaded, she tucked it into her clothing. Loading another box of ammunition and more food into her sack, she returned again to the stable.

She had concealed the sack when Bosky Fulton suddenly came down the ladder and, without glancing at her, went outside and worked his way around to the house.

She recalled hearing a low mutter of conversation from the loft, and remembered that one of the other teamsters was up there.

Fulton remained in the house but, after a few minutes, Rio Hockett came to the door and motioned to one of the other men. The man crawled, then suddenly darted for the door and ducked inside, a bullet tapping the doorjamb with a disgusted finger.

Aided by Laura, Irina returned to the wagons and removed more of the food and ammunition. No shot was fired at them.

Buffalo returned to the stable. "They're pullin' out," he said. "Those smokes are drawin' them off. I'd say we'd better light out of here."

"Do you suppose it is a trick? Something to draw us out of this position?"

"Don't think so. Their dust shows up too far off for that. They've sure enough taken out."

Roy Harding strolled up to the door. "What do you think, Buff? Could we make Fort Cummings? My guess would be the troops are out by this time."

The rest of their party slowly congregated. "Please," Edna Dagget said, "let us go now."

Bosky Fulton spoke from the stable door. "Too late for you folks. You're goin' to stay here. We're takin' out."

Their heads turned as one, and Bosky Fulton stood in the stable door behind them, and beside him were four men with rifles, hip high, ready to fire.

"We decided we don't like it here no more," Fulton said. "Rio, you shuck their guns and shake them down for money or whatever."

"If you wish to leave," Count Henri said coolly, "you must realize you are not alone. We were discussing such a move when you came in. I suggest you harness the teams and be ready to move out."

"We go," Fulton repeated, "you stay."

Von Hallstatt clutched his rifle by the upper barrel, but he stood among the women and there was no chance of bringing it into use without endangering them all. And he had seen how quickly Fulton could go into action.

"If you appear with our belongings," Dagget warned, "questions will be asked. It must be obvious to you that many of our weapons and other belongings will be recognized or easily identified."

Fulton grinned at Dagget. "Not in Mexico. Not in the border towns. And when the Apaches get through with you folks nobody will be asking any questions at all."

He glanced over at Harding. "You're in the wrong crowd, Roy. You belong with us."

"I like it where I am," Harding replied bluntly. "I

never did cotton to thieves. Nor do I want to get my neck stretched."

Fulton shrugged. "Suit yourself. Soon as they see what those smokes meant the Apaches will be back. They'll take care of whatever we leave."

When they had been disarmed, their guns were emptied and handed back. "Look funny if you had no guns. It would make the Apaches talk and we might have to answer to the Army if we were caught. So you just keep those fancy guns."

Irina thought of her derringer. If she could get it out . . . but that would only lead to shooting and her friends would be wounded or killed.

Hockett took their rings from their fingers and what valuables they had on their persons. Cold with anger, Irina watched, knowing the men were as helpless to act as she herself.

The heaviest of the riding stock were hitched to the wagon into which they loaded all that remained of food, ammunition, and valuables that could be disposed of below the border. The horses were not broken to drive, but to men accustomed to the handling of broncos it made no difference. Her own horses were led out and for a moment she felt a savage pleasure. Neither of her horses had ever been ridden by a man, and while these men were horsemen, nonetheless she knew the mares would be watching for an opportunity to throw their riders and escape.

"Leave the roan," Fulton said, "he's all stove up."

"They'll take that horse and hunt for help," Hockett objected.

"Rio, you know that horse is in bad shape. Where would they go for help? The nearest would be seventy or eighty rough miles, maybe twice that far, and Apaches all over the country."

Suddenly Fulton's eyes switched to Irina. "You," he said, "you and that Davis gal. You're a-coming with us."

"I think not."

There was an odd, snakelike quality in the way in which Fulton turned his head.

Count Henri had spoken, and now he met Fulton's gaze calmly. Only a fool could look at the Frenchman and doubt that he would fight.

Roy Harding took a step wide of the group, but in a position that made his intentions obvious. Von Hallstatt gathered himself, giving all his attention to Fulton.

"Ride out with what you have," Henri said coolly, "otherwise you must kill us all, and you'll not do it without our leaving a mark on you.

"I suspect this Colonel Forsyth of whom we have heard will be curious as to why we were all shot at close range and why a wagon is gone. Also," he added, "the Apaches may not be so far away as to wonder why there is shooting when they are not attacking. They might be curious enough to return to find out."

"Forget 'em, Bosky," Hockett said. "We'll find plenty of women in Mexico."

Fulton turned abruptly. "All right, let's go!"

They left in a swirl of dust, and when they were gone, only Roy Harding, Buffalo Harris, and Mako, the cook they had brought from Europe, remained with them.

Irina uncovered the ammunition hidden under a pile of blankets in a corner, and ammunition was passed out among them. The sun was setting.

"We cannot defend this place," von Hallstatt said. "We are too few."

"We'd do better to run for the hills," Harding suggested. "We might find a better place to hole up."

"We'll need water," Buffalo said doubtfully.

———

SHALAKO RODE UP out of the wash and walked the Arab stallion into the circle. "Get whatever grub you've got, blankets and whatever you can carry. If you want to live you've got to get out of here."

"There's water here!" Dagget protested. "And that stable is built like a fort!"

Shalako wasted no words. "How will you get water with Indians shooting into the door?"

"A trip across the desert will kill my wife!" Dagget protested.

"What will happen if she stays here?"

Irina wasted no time listening. Mustering the help of Julia and Laura, they began getting what blankets and food there was. Von Hallstatt and Henri made a stretcher of two long coats by slipping a pole through the arms of the two coats on one side, then another pole on the other. Then they buttoned the coats.

It was quite dark when they finally moved out. Edna Dagget went first, walking beside her husband. The roan followed, led by Julia, and packed with food and medical supplies. The Arab was also loaded down, and led by Laura.

Henri and von Hallstatt carried the stretcher on which Hans lay, protesting the necessity for taking him. Harding and Harris brought up the rear, and Mako walked behind the Arab.

Shalako had removed his boots and donned moccasins

for the walk. They were Apache moccasins that came well up the leg and had stiffer soles for desert walking.

The stars were out, the night very still. Once, three years before, he had camped at the place where he planned to take them. He had no idea of attempting to make Fort Cummings. With the wounded man and Edna Dagget they could not hope to make the distance, and Apaches had been known to kill right under the walls of a fort. Nor would Julia Paige stand up to such a walk . . . the others might.

The journey before them was serious enough without thinking of the much, much longer trek to Fort Cummings.

All he could expect to do was to hide them in the hills and hope the backwash of retreating Apaches did not find them.

Harris had told him briefly about the robbery and flight of the group under Fulton, but that was none of his affair.

Shalako walked to the head of the small column, Irina falling in beside him. Von Hallstatt glanced at them as they went by, but made no comment.

"Why did you come back?" she asked suddenly.

If there was an answer to that he did not know what it was, nor was he a man given to self-analysis or worry about his motives. If they were caught out in the open there was no chance for them, simply none at all.

Knowing no logical answer, he did not attempt to make one, but walked beside her in silence. He walked well ahead of the others so the sounds from the desert would not be merged with their own sounds.

When they halted he fell back and squatted on his heels beside the stretcher, rolling a smoke in the darkness. Carefully shielding the flame, he lighted it, then handed it to Kreuger.

The German inhaled deeply, gratefully. "It is the little things," Kreuger said.

"Yes."

"It is far?"

This man was beyond truth or lies, and he had shown himself a brave man. "It is farther than I told them. You will understand."

"A good place?"

"At the last it will be bad for you, Hans. There will be climbing and turning, but it is a good place."

"Do not think of me."

The bulk of Gillespie Mountain lifted against the sky, still several miles away. The notch toward which he directed their steps was just to the south of it. The cliffs at that place reared up more than a thousand feet and, atop that cliff, between it and Elephant Butte Canyon, there was a place to hide. There was water at the head of Park Canyon and the corner where the two canyons headed up was a difficult place to attack.

"I do not think you have long been a Western man," Kreuger said. "The general was surprised when you mentioned Vegetius and Saxe."

"A Western man is a man from elsewhere," Shalako said. "The West was an empty land and men were drawn to it from the East, from Europe, even from China. An officer killed with Custer at Little Bighorn had been a Papal Guard at the Vatican. I know a rancher in New Mexico who was an officer in Queen Victoria's Coldstream Guards. There is a marshal in the Indian Territory who served in the French Army. Western men were poor men, rich men, beggar men, thieves. Only whatever they were, they were strong men or they did not come West, and of those who came, only the strongest survived."

"And you?"

Faintly, on the soft wind, was a smell of woodsmoke. Shalako swore. "There are Indians south of us."

"And you?" Kreuger persisted.

"A man who wanders, that is what I am. It is a wide land, and much of it I have not seen, and much I wish to see again. A man is what he is, and what he is shows in his actions. I do not ask where a man came from or what he was . . . none of that is important.

"It is what a man does, how he conducts himself that matters, not who his family were." He got up. "I know it is otherwise in Europe."

"Not entirely," Kreuger said, "but it is important." He paused, then added defensively, "Breeding is important."

"Breeding can breed weakness as well as strength, cowardice as well as bravery. I do not think much thought was given to virtue or courage when the bloodlines were laid down. They did not breed for quality, they bred for money. Estates were married, not people."

"There is something in what you say," Kreuger confessed reluctantly.

Walking forward again, he spoke to each of them. "Not a whisper," he said, "not a sneeze. If you drop anything you may drop our lives with it. No matches, no cigarettes . . . there are Indians south of us."

The woodsmoke might come from Cowboy Spring or even that other spring beyond the buttes. Not far enough away for comfort. When they moved out again, Buffalo took the lead and Harding shared the stretcher with Shalako.

Edna Dagget was already dragging her feet. Julia, although she walked well, was showing discomfort.

They walked and rested, they walked again . . . without the stretcher they might have made it by daybreak, as it was a rising wind tuned the violins of the desert shrubs, the Animas Mountains lifted a black wall before them, but a tinge of crimson touched the ridge. Reluctantly the darkness retreated into the narrow-mouthed canyons.

No smoke against the sky. They halted again where mountain run-off had cut a gash in the accumulated debris at the mountains' base. Charles and Edna Dagget huddled together, holding their faces tight against disaster. Laura's eyes seemed larger this morning, and there were hollows in her cheeks.

Only Hans Kreuger seemed unchanged.

Mako, a thin, wiry man who looked more like a doctor of philosophy than a cook, glanced up as Shalako approached him. "I could make some coffee, sir," he suggested.

"No."

Shalako allowed nearly an hour of rest, for the Daggets had little reserve remaining.

It was cold in the shadow of the mountains. The desert lay pale beige before them, dotted with cloud shadow and desert shrubs. Julia Paige looked at the desert and held her shoulders pinched against the chill. Von Hallstatt had a stubble of beard on his jaws, and he stared sullenly at the sand. Count Henri leaned back against the bank, breathing easily.

Shalako squatted on his heels and studied them from under the brim of his hat, assaying the reserves of each.

Von Hallstatt was like iron. Whatever else he was, there

was strength in the man, strength of body and strength of will. The breeding had told there, all right. This was one who had been bred for the Prussian Army officer corps . . . yet the breeding had lost something, too.

Henri . . . a member of the nobility who still possessed nobility. His physical strength might be less, but his morale was greater, he had stamina of the spirit, which outweighs all physical strength.

Shalako was rising to start them moving again when he heard a sound that was more than the wind. Hat off, he lifted his head slowly until his eyes cleared the bank. Not fifty yards away were four Apaches, riding single file.

Naked but for breechclouts, rifles in their hands, they were walking their horses toward the wash in which Shalako stood. Only their line of travel would take them into the wash some fifty or sixty yards ahead of their party. It was Shalako's good luck that their eyes had been averted as his head cleared the edge of the wash.

Von Hallstatt was beside him, and there was no mistaking the look in his eyes as the rifle started to come up. Shalako shoved the rifle barrel down, and the German jerked it from under his hand and started to lift it again. At that instant an Apache looked toward them.

"Let go, you fool!" von Hallstatt whispered. "I am going to kill him."

"What about the women? Do you want to get them killed as well as yourself?"

Their eyes locked and meanwhile the Apaches dipped into the wash ahead of them. They crossed the wash around a slight bend from the waiting party, and neither group could see the other, but they heard the scramble of the horses as they left the wash.

"You put a hand on me again," von Hallstatt said, "and I shall kill you."

"I seen it tried," Buffalo commented.

"You would have killed one Indian," Shalako said, "and then we would have been pinned down without water. Right where we stand it will be more than a hundred degrees within two hours, and maybe ten degrees hotter before the day is out."

"We could have killed them all."

"As long as I am with this party you will be guided by me. If you want to kill Apaches you can go out on your own."

"Take your horse, then," von Hallstatt replied, "and get out of here. We don't need you."

"Frederick!" Irina was appalled.

"If he hadn't interfered we could have killed all four of them," von Hallstatt said angrily.

Shalako gestured toward the mountains. "And what about *them*?"

The German's head snapped around. Along the wall of the mountain, a good half mile away, moved a party of at least eight Indians.

The German's jaw set sullenly, but he said nothing.

"All right," Shalako said, "if you want me to leave, I'll leave. I'll take my horse and ride out of here."

"No, Mr. Carlin," Irina interrupted. "I loaned Mohammet to you. I want you to stay, but if you must go, by all means take him."

"If he goes," Buffalo said, "I go."

"Go, then. And be damned to you!" Von Hallstatt's face was pale with fury.

He could not have said why he was angry. For the first time in his life he was faced with a situation which he could not command. Common sense warned him that Shalako knew far more of what it was necessary to know to save them, but from the first there had been a conflict of personalities coupled with what was undoubtedly jealousy at Irina's seeming interest.

Yet through his anger these threads of reason showed, irritating him all the more.

"I suggest we talk this over," Henri said. "We have much to consider, Frederick."

Roy Harding had been watching von Hallstatt with a curious, unbelieving expression on his face.

"Meaning no disrespect, General von Hallstatt," Kreuger spoke weakly from his stretcher, "but where would we go? What would we do?"

Count Henri arose and walked to the rear end of the stretcher, Harding picked up the front end, and Shalako walked off to the head of the small column. Without further discussion the others fell into place and followed after.

Von Hallstatt looked at them with mingled exasperation and relief. "I have no reasonable alternative," he said, after a minute.

Buffalo Harris had stopped beside him, and together they walked off, bringing up the rear of the column.

They were climbing now, every step an effort, nor did Shalako hold down the pace. He stepped out swiftly, knowing the sooner they got among the rocks or in some kind of cover the better off they would be. The nakedness of the desert was appalling, and he had seen a detachment of troops surrounded and picked off one by one in such a position as theirs.

Irina kept pace with him but only with an effort, and

it was only the lure of the shade offered by the canyons that kept her going.

Edna Dagget fell down. She was helped up by her husband, who half-carried her as they continued. Julia was lagging, and she had torn her skirt on a cactus thorn.

Several times they made brief stops, and then when Gillespie Mountain loomed to their north, Shalako stopped in the shade of a cliff. To the south the wall of the mountain reared up a thousand feet, not sheer, but incredibly steep.

"We will go up there," Shalako said.

Von Hallstatt glanced at the cliff, then looked over at Shalako, completely incredulous. Irina was appalled.

"It will be pretty rough going," Shalako admitted, "but there's a makeshift of a trail. I'll take Count Henri and go up first. We will need a man with a rifle up there to cover our climb."

"Why not me?" Irina suggested. "I can't help with Hans, but I can use a rifle."

It was a logical suggestion, and he had thought of it. "You will be up there alone," he said. "I've got to come back down."

"I've been alone before."

"As you wish."

Hitching his pack into position, he took up his Winchester and started for the trail, and Irina fell in behind him. Von Hallstatt threw his pack on the ground and spat.

Buffalo glanced at him and, catching Harding's eyes, he shrugged.

Walking into the maze of rocks, Shalako ducked under a slab, entering a narrow space between boulders. They emerged in a narrow watercourse and beside it a trail.

"Sheep trail," Shalako commented. "Bighorns."

Once he started to climb, he walked slowly, for he had climbed often and knew that only a fool hurries. The narrow trail switched and doubled. The sheep had used it single file, and it was incredibly narrow. The sun was blazing hot, and when her hand accidentally touched a rock, she jerked it away with a gasp. It was hot enough to fry eggs.

Here and there Shalako paused to move rocks from the trail or to widen it for those who would follow. Then the trail jogged a little and briefly they would be in the shade of the cliff.

Shalako stopped and removed his hat, peering at the trail ahead, and wiping the sweatband. Irina was flushed and panting, glad of the momentary respite.

"Will they find our trail?"

"They'll find it."

"Have you lived in the West all your life?"

He glanced at her, faint humor lurking in his eyes. "It's a good country," he said, "and a beautiful country. It's an easy country to get lost in."

"If one has reason to get lost."

He smiled. "Yes, if one has reason. Or if one doesn't." He gestured, "It's a big country, and a lot of men have come West their folks never heard of again. Some were killed, some died, some made new lives for themselves and wanted no part of what they left behind. Some men find out here the answer to all they need."

"And you?"

"It's a big country, and I like it. A man has room to think out there, and room to move. I'm a man who doesn't like to be crowded."

"And what of the future?"

"Ah . . . the future? Yes, there's always that. Someday I must sit down and think it all out, but perhaps I shall take up some land, build the kind of house I want, and raise some cattle, breed a few horses." He got up. "You took a risk coming into this country with a stallion like Mohammet. To say nothing of those mares."

He took up his rifle. "It is a thing I've noticed, Miss Carnarvon, the first generation out here want horses that will stand the gaff, stand up to brutal work and hard riding, the second generation are already thinking of horses that look like something, and the next generation will only want fancy horses and all the elaborate leather and silver they can get on them."

He started off, and she followed. A moment later she paused, and he stopped. She eased her foot inside her boot, then started on. "You have no silver on your saddle," she said.

"I'm from the first generation," he said, "and silver reflects sunlight. Nobody but a fool wants flashing metal on his gear or a white horse in this country. Too many folks can know when you're coming."

They skirted the edge of a cliff that fell away for several hundred feet, wedged themselves between boulders, and then suddenly emerged on top.

"You will never get the horses up that trail," she said. "No kind of a horse could get between those rocks."

"I'm going to ride around . . . and it is a long way around."

The air was surprisingly cool. A faint breeze smelled of pines and cedars. Facing south she overlooked the deep gash of Elephant Butte Canyon. Park Canyon, starting almost at her feet, pointed away toward the southwest. The point of land on which they stood was but a few acres in extent, and there were scattered pines, some cedar, and a few shrubs of which she knew nothing. They were the dry, harsh-looking shrubs of the desert mountains. There was also a little grass.

"Wait at the top of the trail," he told her, "but do not be distracted by what is happening on the trail itself. They will get up somehow and that is not your problem.

"Watch the desert, watch all the approaches to the trail below. Do not fire unless necessary, but if they start toward the foot of the trail, stop them."

"Is there danger behind us? From the south?"

"You never know, so you had better keep a careful lookout."

He discarded his pack, leaving it beside her. "I will be going down."

"Why are you doing this? You were clear of it, you were away, you were free. And sometimes I think you do not even like us."

"Shooting downhill that way . . . it can throw you off your target."

"You didn't answer me."

"Does a man have to have a reason? Maybe it is because you loaned me a horse." He paused at the trail's head and pointed off through the trees to the southwest. "You watch for me there. I'll come up west of that small canyon. But don't take it for granted that whoever comes will be me, and I won't come in the night.

"I'll identify myself, so be careful."

"It is good of you to help us, Mr. Carlin. Especially when Frederick has been so difficult."

He threw a quizzical glance at her. "I don't blame him. If I had a girl as lovely as you, I'd be careful, too. I wouldn't want her traipsing around the country with a strange man."

"Maybe he trusts me."

"Doesn't look like it. Anyway, it isn't a matter of trusting. Maybe he's afraid I'll just take you and run, leave them all to the desert."

"I'd have something to say about that." She looked at him boldly. "Are you trying to frighten me?" She paused. "After all, I am practically engaged to Frederick."

"Doesn't mean a thing."

He started to walk away, and she looked after him. "Frederick has been difficult," she added.

When he said nothing, but started down the trail, she called after him, "And you're difficult, Mr. Carlin!"

She had no idea whether he heard her or not. She heard his footsteps on the trail, and then they faded, and she was alone. Wind stirred in the cedars, and there was no other sound for a long time.

The air was very clear. She looked north up the wide valley toward the ranch they had left. Dancing heat waves cut off the view in the distance along the foot of the mountains.

Shalako . . . it was a strange name, an exciting name. And he was an exciting man. Exciting, yet strangely calming at such times as this, for he seemed so completely in command of the situation . . . not that any person could be sure of coming out alive from such an ordeal, but she had the feeling that if they failed, if Shalako ever failed in such a situation as this, it would only be after everything possible had been done.

What there was to do, he would do; what there was to consider, he would have considered.

She had told him she was almost engaged to Frederick. Now why had she said *that*? It was not true. There was a sort of understanding between them, but nothing had been said, not really. She knew that Frederick wanted to marry her, and she knew she had been considering it.

And now Shalako.

But how could she consider him at all? How would he look among her friends in London? His weather-beaten features, his big, strong hands, that shaggy, powerful look he had about him.

No, he would not fit.

Or would he? Some of the soldiers from the Northwest Frontier of India were like that . . . not shaggy, however. But a haircut would take care of that.

But why consider his coming to her life? And what made her believe he would be happy there?

No, this was his country, this was his land, and it was a strong, beautiful land. She inhaled deeply. There was something about the mountain air that made one want to inhale deeply . . . it was like fresh, clear, cold water in the throat.

———

BUFFALO HARRIS WAS the last man up the trail. At the last, when Harris waited to follow the others, he stood for a minute or two finishing a cigarette with Shalako.

"Along the east side of the mountains they rise up steep and high for several miles, so I'm going on up this canyon we're in and strike the head of Wolf Canyon. There's an old Indian trail running back toward the southeast from there, and a fork in that will take me right into the park."

"You take care. I don't cotton to that general."

"He's a good man, Buff. Just out of his element, that's all. Don't worry about him."

He watched Buffalo start up the cliff, then picked up the roan's lead rope and mounted the stallion. It was very hot, and weariness suddenly flooded over him. Just as the long, hot ride had taken its toll from the roan, it was now getting to him. It had been a long time since he had been this tired.

Squinting his eyes under the pulled-down hatbrim, he studied the terrain with care. Nothing must happen to him, for he carried nearly all the food and ammunition for the party.

Behind him was the Playas Valley, before him, beyond the mountains, was the Animas Valley. He started Mohammet, walking the stallion out of the copse where they had assembled for the climb, and he turned the Arab westward.

The sun burned on his back, and his eyelids were heavy. His eyes ached and the lids burned with staring over the wide, hot spaces. There was no sound but the hoof-falls of his horses, the creak of the saddle. He touched his tongue to his dry lips and mopped his forehead with the sleeve of his shirt.

He topped out on the rise, and Wolf Canyon lay before him. He came down off the ridge and in the brief shadow of the boulders, he studied the terrain again. It was hard to focus his eyes, but he took his time, measuring the sunlit vastness before him, the great shoulders of raw, red rock, the splashes of green, the great, broken, shattered land.

A lizard darted out on a rock near him, and stopped, its side panting with the heat. Overhead a buzzard circled, but the blue sky of morning was gone, and in its place was a sky of heat-misted brass from which the sun blazed. He rubbed the stubble on his jaws, and started the Arab forward, feeling his way down the slope, watching for the trail he knew was there.

———

UPON A SHOULDER of Gillespie Mountain, *Tats-ah-das-ay-go* turned his cold eyes toward the southwest . . . movement! Something stirred among the sunlit hills.

Squatted in the shadow of a rock, the Quick-Killer's eyes held upon the far distant hill. The movement had been there, and then it was gone . . . it had been no sheep, and nothing else would be large enough.

Again!

He squinted his eyes against the glare. A man. A rider with two horses. Swiftly, he turned and went down off the mountain to his horse.

Let Chato go his way . . . let Loco and the others go . . . he would find his own kills, and leave them where he found them.

———

FAR AND AWAY to the south and east, along the foot of the Big Hatchet Mountains, Rio Hockett led the stolen wagon and its cargo. Bob Marker rode beside him.

Flanking the wagon were two riders, and two men rode the seat of the wagon. Two more brought up the rear, riding wide of the wagon to be free of its dust. Two more rode inside, armed and ready. Bosky Fulton brought up the rear, nor was it by accident that he chose the position.

They had seen no Apaches, nor any Indian sign at all. Rio Hockett was walking his horse and well out in the lead with Marker when he smelled dust. Drawing up sharply, he turned in his saddle. No wind was blowing.

Uneasily, he looked around him. Nothing stirred. The smell of dust was gone. He looked across toward the Animas Mountains, but saw nothing. Nearby were several drowned peaks, almost buried in the sand that would eventually cover them.

Hockett mopped his brow and looked around him again. Bob Marker, a mean-looking Missourian, shot him a sharp glance. "What's the matter?"

"I don't like the feel of things. I thought I smelled dust."

"Our own, prob'ly. Let's go. There's water south of them peaks, and Mexico not far beyond it."

"Bosky wants us to go east toward Juarez . . . not a bad idea. Say! I know a little Mex gal in Juarez, who—"

And then he saw the tracks.

Hockett turned swiftly, slapping spurs to his horse, and started for the wagon. He saw it swing broadside, saw a man fall from the wagon seat into the sand, and then he heard the report of a gun . . . seconds later there were other shots.

He glanced around for Marker and saw his horse running riderless, stirrups flapping. He felt his own horse go under him and kicked his feet free of the stirrups, dropping like an acrobat even as his horse went head over heels. He turned in his tracks, firing his rifle from the hip.

Hockett was a big man, and tough. He had been a buffalo hunter, a cow thief, and a scalp hunter, and he had nerve. Levering the Winchester, he fired again and again. He got one, saw another stagger. He hosed bullets at them . . . too fast.

The Winchester clicked on an empty chamber and he dropped it, drawing both guns. Something jerked at his sleeve, sand kicked against his boots. He saw a horse fall, heard a shrill scream of pain from behind him, and he thumbed back the hammer of the .44, firing coolly.

There was no doubt in his mind. With shocking clarity, he realized this was the end.

A bullet smashed into his shoulder, turning him half around. He dropped his gun, but with a border shift tossed the gun from hand to hand, then fired again. He stood, spraddle-legged atop a hummock of sand, his long hair blowing wild, a splash of blood across his face from a split scalp.

A bullet knocked a leg from under him, and on one knee he calmly fed shells into the gun. His shoulder was hurting, but he could still use it, so no bone was broken. Behind him there were yells, screams of anguish, and the crackle of flames.

Now a dozen Indians surrounded him, baiting him as they might have baited a wounded bear. He mopped the blood from his face, holding his fire.

His horse was down not far away and his canteen was on the saddle. The distance to the rocks was no more than thirty yards. Straightening to his feet, he limped and staggered to the horse for the canteen and slung it over his shoulder.

Glancing around, he saw the wagon top ablaze, and the bodies of the others scattered around, festooned with arrows. Indians were looting the wagon before the burning canvas fell in upon it.

Taking up his rifle, he merely glanced at the Indians, who watched him curiously. Then he started toward the rocks.

He understood them, he thought bitterly, and he knew they would wait, just as he in their place might have waited. They would allow him to get close to the rocks, almost to safety, before they opened fire.

So he must judge. He walked on, his back muscles held tight against the expected bullets. One step . . . two . . . three.

He broke into a plunging run, staggering and falling, dragging his injured leg.

He managed at least three steps before every rifle smashed lead at him, every arrow sought him.

Yet he made it to the rocks, pierced through and through with bullets and arrows, and then fell into a crevice among the rocks. In the last moment before he toppled into the rocks he turned on them and opened fire, emptying his pistols. And then he fell.

An Apache, riding close, thrust a spear into his side.

And then they left him alone, for they knew he would not move again and they would return for his weapons when they had looted his wagon.

He coughed blood, lying jammed among the rocks, and once he opened his eyes to look up at the wide sky. Like Bob Marker, Rio Hockett had been a Missourian, and when only a youngster he had ridden on a couple of raids with Bloody Bill Anderson, riding with a young horse thief with red-rimmed eyes who kept batting his lids named Dingus James. Jesse James, they called him later.

The sky looked the same as in the days when he had plowed a straight furrow back on the farm . . . he had never plowed one since.

He coughed again, and closed his eyes. There was so much pain that he hardly felt any of it at all, but he could hear the Indians shouting and laughing as they pulled the rest of the supplies from the wagon.

Suddenly he felt a tug at his belt, and opening his eyes he looked up at Bosky Fulton.

Fulton was holding a finger to his lips, but seemed unharmed. Swiftly and roughly, Fulton pulled Hockett's gun belt loose, then took his gun and what remained of his belongings. With no thought for the pain he might cause by the rough handling, he turned the wounded man roughly this way and that, going through his pockets.

Hockett grasped at Fulton's sleeve with fingers that no longer had the strength to grasp, but Fulton brushed them aside, and then he was gone. Hockett tried to call after him, but no sound came, and then he died.

Fulton had been hanging back when the wagon was attacked, and in the first flurry of movement, he took to the rocks and fired no shot that would attract attention to him. He abandoned his friends without hesitation, and remained in the rocks until the shooting was over, then crawled out to get Hockett's weapons and ammunition.

Returning to his horse he led the animal farther away, then waited. In his pockets he had most of the money and the best of the jewels taken from the hunting party, which he had held pending a division in Mexico. It was not, he decided, a bad deal. The rest of them were dead, and instead of going to Juarez, he would go west to Tucson and San Francisco.

At approximately the same time that Shalako took leave of Buffalo Harris, Bosky Fulton was searching for a trail through the same mountains from the east, and shortly after sundown he turned his horse into the same trail as that on which Shalako rode.

Ten miles or more divided them, and each made dry camp, each went to sleep without food. Bosky Fulton in a small clump of brush, Shalako behind the ruined adobe.

———

BEYOND THE HATCHET Mountains, Lieutenant Hall, with a small detachment of troops from Fort Cummings, made a fireless bivouac. West of the Animas Mountains, bound for Stein's Pass, Lieutenant McDonald camped with his Indian scouts and one corporal. To the north, not yet in the arena of action, Lieutenant Colonel "Sandy" Forsyth camped with some four hundred men of the Fourth Cavalry.

There had been a big fight at San Carlos, and now the scattered bands of the Apache were gathering under their three leaders, Chato, Loco, and Nachita. They were perfectly aware of McDonald's presence and that he had with him a number of Yuma and Mohave scouts, including Yuma Bill.

The Apaches had fled south from San Carlos, while Forsyth had come west from Fort Cummings. The Apaches, who usually know everything in the desert, did not know this. Their scouts had seen McDonald's small force, and they knew of Hall . . . of Forsyth they knew nothing.

———

IN THE SMALL area at the head of the canyons, Buffalo Harris argued for small fires, carefully shielded, and he kept them together in the most defensible position he could find.

Von Hallstatt spread his blankets and stretched out, dead beat. He had expected nothing like this. When attacked, he had believed they would be mass attacks of running, easily killed savages, and instead there had been few targets, those few fleeting and gone. Deserted by his teamsters, he was here, where he had never expected to be, moving at the whim of a man he scarcely knew and profoundly disliked.

Thinking of the Indians irritated him, for it brought to mind an almost forgotten lecture heard while still a cadet, when they were told that all warfare would be revised, influenced by the fighting on the American frontier.

The warfare of the future, they were told, meant aimed rifle fire, mobility, infiltration, and individual enterprise. The idea had been unpalatable to the students, and they had rejected it en masse, for it meant initiative by the individual soldier, and seemed to imply less control from the top.

Von Hallstatt lay with his hands clasped behind his head and coldly appraised the situation as it had taken place at the ranch. Despite superior fire power, superior weapons, and perhaps superior marksmanship, they had been immobilized and rendered incapable of counterattack.

For the first time he had faced an enemy who was virtually invisible, an enemy who knew and utilized the terrain.

Despite his unfamiliarity with the country and Indian warfare in general, he was beginning to see how a small, well-trained force, virtually living off the country, could defeat or at least nullify the efforts of a much larger and better equipped command. It was his first experience with guerrilla warfare, and the very idea of war conducted on such principles made his gorge rise.

War under such conditions was no longer a gentleman's game. It became harsh, practical, and utterly realistic business. Firing in volleys as at a massed enemy front was absurd, for there was no enemy front, the enemy was a shadow, a will-o'-the-wisp.

Frederick von Hallstatt was nothing if not a realist. Lying stretched on his back, staring up at the stars, he considered the situation. Encumbered by the women there was nothing they could do but hope for the arrival of the Army . . . the very Army he had often ridiculed for being unable to dispose of a pack of naked savages.

The chances of getting out were small indeed. The food supply was low. There was ammunition enough for a good long fight, and small chance of worry on that score, but the food they carried could last them only three days, four at the most.

Despite his resentment of Shalako, it was obvious they could not survive without him. Even Buffalo admitted that Shalako was much more familiar with the country and the Indians than anyone else.

This very trip to America had been less for the purpose of hunting big game than for an opportunity to fight Indians. He admitted to himself what he had not admitted to anyone else, although he had jestingly commented on hoping for a brush with the Apaches. Well, he was having it. And so far he had acquitted himself very poorly indeed.

He was a superb rifle shot, yet he had killed but one Indian in all the rounds he had fired. Moreover, he had a feeling the Apaches were shooting more effectively than he, for there had been at least twenty extremely narrow misses back at the ranch; at least twenty times when bullets had come within fractions of an inch of hitting him.

Firelight flickered on the under branches of the surrounding pines, reflected from the smooth faces of the rocks. The air was scented with pine and cedar, and the fire crackled and sparked as it burned pine and needles.

A quail called, and far off, a lone coyote cried his

immeasurable woe to the starlit sky. Buffalo Harris knelt by the fire, feeding its hungry flames with sticks gathered from under the trees. Irina placed the coffeepot on a flat stone, close to the flames.

"I've set some snares," Buffalo commented. "In the morning we may have a rabbit or two."

"Where is he now?"

Buffalo stretched his big hands toward the warmth of the flames in a timeless gesture of devotion to the gods of fire. He waited while the flames seared the few drops of spilled water from the outside of the coffeepot.

"Sleepin', most likely. He's a man sets store by sleep, although I never knew a man to get less of it."

"What's he like? I mean, beyond what you see?"

"He's an uncommon hard man to read. Leaves mighty little sign, no matter how you study his trail."

"Has he been married?"

"Now as to that I couldn't say. Kind of doubt it. Womenfolks take to him. I've seen that aplenty. And he's uncommon gentle with them, although I doubt he'd be that way if they crossed him.

"You'd look long to find a man who knows wild country better, and he tracks like any Apache. He can live off less and travel farther than anybody except maybe an Indian.

"One time I saw a book of this here poetry in his saddle-bag. Near wore out from reading. Of course, that doesn't spell, because out here a man gets so hungry for reading he'll read anything in print. I've lived in bunkhouses where the cowhands used to see who had memorized the most labels off tin cans . . . and any book or paper is read until it's wore out."

"Where's he from?"

Buffalo glanced at her. "Question we never ask out here. We count a man as one who stands up when trouble shows, and we never look to see how much of a shadow a man cast back home. You can't wash gold with water that's run off down the hill."

Von Hallstatt had come up to the fire. "Tradition is important," he said quietly, "and a man has a right to be proud of what he has been and what his family have been."

"Maybe so," Buffalo acknowledged, "but out here we feel we're starting tradition and not living on it. One time you folks in Europe founded families and shaped a tradition, and I've no doubt they were strong men who did it." He got to his feet. "We're making our own traditions now, founding families, building a country.

"We don't figure a man's past is important. We want to know what he is now. The fact that his great-granddaddy was a fightin' man won't kill any Indians today.

"A man starting into wild country wants a man riding beside him that he can depend on. We're a sight more interested in red blood out here than in blue blood, and believe me, General, the two don't always run together."

Buffalo added fuel to the fire. The wood was very dry and burned with a hot, eager flame and little smoke. He accepted a cup of coffee from Irina, tasted it, and said, "Ma'am, you make a man's cup of coffee. Never figured it of you . . . you so stylish and all."

"I learned to cook over a campfire when I was twelve. My father often took me hunting with him."

"That there's the way it should be. A woman should know how to cook and do for a man."

"Does Shalako think that?"

"He's a puzzlin' man, like I said. Who knows what he

thinks? But he's a man to have on your side in a difficulty, and addicted to sudden violence when wrongfully opposed." He sipped coffee. "He favors desert and mountains more than towns."

"Is he running from something?" Von Hallstatt was irritated that the conversation should have turned to Carlin.

"Whatever else may have happened, I strongly doubt Shalako ever ran from anything. He's a most stubborn man when it comes to troublesome times."

"Whatever he is," von Hallstatt said stiffly, "he will be well paid for whatever he does for us."

"Meanin' no offense, General, but if it wasn't for the ladies I reckon you'd all be dead by now. He's of the opinion that every man should fight his own battles and saddle his own broncs. You can lay a bet he's never given a thought to payment."

Buffalo wiped off his mustache with the back of his hand. "Obliged for the coffee, ma'am. I'll be getting out where I can smell Indian."

When he had gone, Irina glanced at von Hallstatt. "Frederick, be careful about offering money. These men have a pride every bit as stiff-necked as your own. You must not offer money to Shalako."

"Perhaps not." He took the coffee she offered. "The man gets my back up. I have no idea why, but it is so. I went to school in England as you know, and always got along fine with the British, but these Americans . . . I cannot like them."

"You are not accustomed to independence in men you think your inferiors, Frederick. I think, perhaps, that is the reason."

"No . . . no, it is something else. I confess that disturbs me in some of the others, but somehow"—he was surprised to realize this was true—"somehow I never thought of him as an inferior."

He tasted the coffee. "It *is* good coffee, Irina. You continue to surprise me." Then he added, "The man has education, undoubtedly a military education."

It was her turn to be surprised. "I was not aware of that."

"The names of Vegetius, Saxe, and Jomini are not as familiar to you as to me, nor are they familiar to the average educated man. They speak of specialization."

"Hans said something to that effect, but he may merely have read the books."

"Possibly. As Harris has said, he is a puzzling man." He glanced at Irina. "And one not to underestimate in any respect."

Irina kept her eyes on the fire, a little startled by the implication. A few days ago she would have been merely amused at the implication that she might be interested in such a man as Shalako Carlin. Now she was no longer sure.

"If we are fortunate, Frederick, we will be far away from here in a few days. Then I doubt if we shall ever see him again . . . or any of these people not of our own group."

"Perhaps." He sounded doubtful, and he was not a man to be uncertain of anything, especially of himself or any situation in which he was involved.

She pushed some sticks farther into the fire and watched the sparks fly upward. How much their lives had changed! Hans was dying . . . Frederick was less arrogant than at any time since she had known him . . . and she herself? Had she changed?

Von Hallstatt got his rifle and moved out to the perimeter of the camp, and Laura came to the fire from Kreuger's bedside.

"He's asleep, I think. Sometimes it is hard to tell . . . he makes believe so we will not feel it necessary to remain at his side."

"Strange, that it should be him. Frederick said two of the wounds were enough to kill him, each in itself. I don't know how he has lived so long."

Laura was silent, and then she said, "Irina . . . I like this . . . the desert, the fire, the stars. If the situation was different, I could love it."

"So could I. Once when I was in Africa with Father, we were camped away out on the veldt, just a small group of us. It was a lovely night. I remember him saying that he would like never to go back."

"It all seems far away." Laura looked thoughtfully at her friend. "You've changed, Irina. It seems so impossible that it was just the day before yesterday that all this started."

"Your father will be worried."

"I hope we'll be safe before he hears about it. He didn't want me to come." She glanced at Irina again. "Father didn't take to Frederick. Thought he was too stiff-necked."

"He isn't, really. And he's lost a lot of what he did have, these past few days."

"Are you going to marry him?"

Irina seated herself on the log near the fire and carefully spread her skirt over her knees. "I don't know, Laura. I really don't know."

"Shalako?"

"That's silly, isn't it? We come from different worlds, we live in different ways, we think differently. The whole idea is absurd."

"With a man like that? Not to me, it isn't. Anyway, I've heard you say many times that you had no desire to live in London or Paris . . . that you wanted an estate in the country. So why not a cattle ranch in New Mexico or Arizona?"

"That's foolish, and you know it."

The night was cool and, above all, singularly still. Beyond the light of the fire the night was a curtain of darkness.

Count Henri came in from the edge of camp and poured a cup of coffee. "It is too quiet," he said, "I don't like it. It reminds me too much of Africa."

He sipped his coffee. "They are out there, I think. I think they are very close to us."

"I wish Shalako would come back," Laura said.

He glanced at her. "So do I, Laura. So do I."

Shalako Carlin bedded down on a patch of sparse, coarse grass well hidden by brush back of the ruined adobe cabin.

Originally built of rock, the cabin had evidently fallen to ruin, and then had been rebuilt with adobe bricks, and had now fallen to ruin again. But despite the shelter offered, he had no intention of being caught within the walls, preferring freedom of movement.

Mohammet, stripped of saddle and bridle, was picketed on the rank grass of a slope just behind him. The night was still, and Shalako was dead tired . . . he fell asleep at once.

An owl hooted from a nearby tree, and a pack rat

cowered at the sound, then sniffed curiously in the direction of the sleeping man.

Out in the forest a pinecone fell and the owl took off on lazy wings through the dark aisles of the scattered trees. The pack rat, relieved, moved hesitantly from the shelter of the catclaw, circled the small clearing and disappeared on some nocturnal business of his own. A bat poised, fluttering dark wings in the air above the ruin, then swooped off, pursuing insects, and there was no other sound but the horse cropping grass. The stars hung their bright lanterns in a dark, still sky and the slight breeze carried a scent of pines along the high ridges.

A long time later, and far out among the trees, sound suddenly seemed to hesitate, and then for a moment there was silence. The stallion's head came up alertly, ears pricked, and the man Shalako opened his eyes, and lay still, listening.

His guns were at hand, but he ignored them, reaching for his knife. He held the blade ready, cutting edge turned up . . . only a fool stabs down with a knife. There is too much bone structure in the upper part of the body . . . unless a man can find that particular vital spot. Holding the knife low, edge upward, one strikes at the soft parts of the body where no bones deflect the blow.

No sound . . . time went by, but he did not relax. Suddenly, the stallion drew back sharply and snorted, and Shalako smelled the Apache. It was a smell of woodsmoke, buckskin, and something acrid, strange . . . a shadow moved . . . lunged.

Shalako rolled to his knees. Unable to judge the position of the Indian in the darkness, he risked everything and slashed across in front of him, and felt the tip of the blade catch flesh. There was a muffled gasp and an iron grip seized his wrist.

Using the powerful muscles of his bent legs, Shalako straightened sharply, jerking the arm up and tearing it free. Instantly he smashed down with a closed fist and felt it *thud* against flesh.

The Indian lunged at him, his knife point tearing Shalako's shirt. Shalako lunged in turn, missed, and the Indian seized his knife arm and tried to throw him over his shoulder. Instantly Shalako threw himself in the direction the Indian was throwing him, bunching his knees under him.

The sudden moving weight threw the Indian forward off balance and he fell on his face with Shalako's knees riding his shoulders. Slippery as greased flesh can be, the Apache slid from under Shalako and came to his feet. Shalako rose with him and thrust home with the knife.

The blade took the Indian under the arm and went all the way in, and Shalako felt the warm gush of blood over his hand as he drew back on the knife. The Indian uttered a low cry and fell backward.

Shalako stepped back, catching his breath, and talking softly to quiet the frightened stallion. He stood perfectly still, watching the dark blotch where the Apache had fallen. He could hear the rasping gasps of the dying man, but he was not trusting the sound, and he waited.

Apparently the lone Apache had been left without a horse by some action of which Shalako knew nothing, and had hoped to get both horse and weapons from him. Yet it worried him that the Indian should be here. Had he been followed? Or had the Indian come upon his trail by accident?

After several minutes had passed and he heard no further sounds, he dropped to his haunches and struck a shielded match.

The Apache was short, powerfully built—and dead.

That first, blind blow with the knife had caught the Indian's shoulder, then cut across his throat, tearing a razor-like gash that covered the Apache with blood.

A relatively new breech-loading Springfield lay on the ground nearby, an Army rifle. The Apache wore an Army belt and an ammunition pouch. The rifle stock was hand-buffed and could not have been out of the soldier's hands for more than a few days, perhaps only a few hours. That stock had been given loving care by a man who appreciated fine wood, something with which no Apache would have bothered.

So the Army was in the field, and probably not far away. If so the possibilities were that Chato was in full flight toward the border, but avid for rapine and murder, hungry for horses and loot.

Untying the stallion, he saddled up, and, sliding the extra rifle into the boot, he checked the loads on his own Winchester '76. The first gray was lightening the eastern sky when he crossed the saddle into Wolf Canyon.

———

TEN MILES TO the south and east, Bosky Fulton turned on his side and opened his eyes. He got up, absentmindedly brushing needles and grass from his clothing, while listening for what the predawn had to offer. It was time to be moving.

He was irritable and worried. The country would be alive with Indians, and he decided his best route would be toward Stein's Pass. Yet he was uneasy, and even after he had saddled up, he did not at once move out.

For the first time he had something to lose, and it worried him. He had money and jewels enough to make him a moderately rich man, and he intended a wild time in San Francisco.

He was somewhere southeast and mostly east of Animas Peak, and the thought of crossing Animas Valley worried him. The valley was a wide-open route south into Sonora and Chihuahua, and a logical route for the Apaches to take. The trail near which he had bedded down led right into the Animas Valley.

He waited a long time, then led his horse forward and waited again. After a while he stepped into the saddle and rode out into the narrow trail. He was somewhere near Walnut Creek, and there was still some distance to go before reaching the valley.

Bosky Fulton scratched warily under his arm and looked cautiously around. He had a way of turning his head without moving his shoulders, dropping his head forward and looking around over his shoulder from the corners of his eyes. He was worried and wary. He recalled all too well a time when he had found two teamsters tied head down to the rear wheels of their wagon. Low fires had been built under their heads. It was an old Apache trick.

Scared? He was scared all right. No man in his right mind rode through Apache country and was not scared. He was scared, all right, but he was ready, too.

That Carnarvon woman . . . he thought of her suddenly. By the Lord Harry he'd like to—

There would be plenty of women in San Francisco and with the money he had, he could pick and choose.

He walked his horse slowly forward, touching his dry lips with his tongue.

Some miles ahead of him, the Apache known as *Tats-ah-das-ay-go* slid down from the rocks to a point behind the ruined cabin. He found where the stallion had been tied, and he found the dead Apache.

He stared down at him with contempt. He had attacked a sleeping man and had been killed!

Tats-ah-das-ay-go squatted on his heels against the cabin wall and smoked, and as he smoked he read the signs left by Shalako and the Apache with the ease of a man reading print.

The white-eyes had awakened, or had been lying awake. He could see where his knees had been and where his feet had pushed off as he lunged, and the fighting had taken place a few feet away from where the white-eyes had slept.

He left small trail, this white-eyes, and he slept lightly. He was a warrior, and he wore moccasins, Apache moccasins . . . perhaps he had lived among them? To kill such a man would be a great feat. *Tats-ah-das-ay-go* got to his feet and returned among the rocks to his horse.

Yes, a great feat . . .

CHAPTER 4

I T WAS NOON of April 22, two days after the San Carlos fight, that Lieutenant Hall cut the trail of the von Hallstatt party.

Trailing the wagons, the lieutenant came upon the deserted ranch where the remains of the fight lay all about. His scouts worked out a puzzling story that to some extent coincided with his own observations.

There had been a fight with the Apaches; one dead Apache was found within the wagon circle. Apparently the defense had been successful for the wagons had not been looted by Apaches . . . that was obvious from things left behind.

Whoever looted them had made a systematic search for valuables, passing up many things any Apache would have taken. And the Apaches would have carried away the body of their dead warrior.

"Two parties left here, Lieutenant. The first party with most of the horses and one wagon headed south toward the border. The other bunch with two horses and one man carried in a stretcher—wounded man, most likely—cut off southwest."

He indicated the broken boards of an ammunition box. "I count enough shells for one used-up box. They made a fight of it, then there must have been trouble among them.

"The wagon had four horses hitched to it, and, by their

hoofs, small stock. Riding stock, more'n likely. Four of the men with that wagon had flat-heeled boots . . . teamsters, I take it."

"Well, what do you think?"

The scout squatted on his heels, considered a minute, then spat into the sand. "Thievery, that's what I think. That damn' fool Fritz come a high-tailing it into this country with a pack of no-account thieves.

"Rio Hockett never did have no brains. Nervy man, but bullheaded and no-account. I take it he and his crowd helped fight off the Indians, then looted the wagons and pulled out for Mexico."

Lieutenant Hall considered the situation, then mounted his troop and rode off on the trail of the wagon.

By midafternoon they had come up to the wagon. It had been looted and burned, and all about lay the mutilated bodies of the slain men. The lieutenant or the trackers knew most of them by name, and the last one to be found was Hockett.

"Good riddance," Lieutenant Hall said briefly, "the man was a thief and a troublemaker."

"He made a fight of it," the scout said, indicating the brass shells lying about. "Now here's an odd thing . . . his gun belt is gone. Taken by somebody who came up behind the rocks." The scout pointed to the heelprint of a boot. "I'd say that was Fulton. Didn't see his body down there, and if anybody would get out of a mess-up like this here, it would be Bosky."

"He got away?" Lieutenant Hall was incredulous.

"Sure as shootin'. Man had small feet, and so had Fulton. Seen his track many a time. Him an' Hockett run together, an' bad as Hockett was, he was tame stuff to Fulton."

"He will have to get on as best he can," the lieutenant said briefly. "We must find the hunting party."

Turning north, they skirted the Hatchets. With luck they would cut the trail of the party with the wounded man and the women. Such a group had small chance of survival, and the mystery remained. Why had they turned south?

"They've got a man with them who didn't start with them," the scout said. "Counting the bodies back there and what we found at the ranch, I figure Harding and Harris stayed with the Eastern party, but there's another man."

"Wells, what about Wells?"

"Could be. Don't act like him though."

Miles away, beyond two valleys and the Animas Range, another situation was developing.

Lieutenant McDonald halted his command. It was very hot. Dust arose from every step the horses took and when the troop halted the dust cloud drifted over them and settled upon their clothing, their faces, and in their nostrils. Aside from himself, all were Yuma or Mohave Indians except for the corporal, a stocky man with a beet-red face, and a veteran soldier.

The lieutenant's mission: to find Indian trails recently made, to locate raiding Apaches and report to the main body under Colonel Forsyth. No man was better qualified for the job, nor was any man more conscientious in performance of his duty.

At this moment, Lieutenant McDonald was worried. So far he had found no tracks, but three days had transpired since the San Carlos attack, and the air smelled of trouble. The fact that he had seen no Apaches was no consolation, for he lived by the old rule: When you see

Apaches, be afraid; and when you can see no Apaches, be twice as afraid.

Fear was not a thing of which to be ashamed unless a man let fear conquer him. Fear could be a spur to action and a safeguard against carelessness. McDonald had helped to bury a good many soldiers who were reckless or took unnecessary risks.

Yuma Bill, who rode beside him, pointed toward the Pelonchillo Mountains, his face as dark and craggy as the mountains he indicated. "I think," he suggested, as he pointed.

"We'll have a look, Bill."

McDonald lighted his pipe. Why he wanted it at all he did not know, for the smoke was dry and hot, and his uniform smelled of stale tobacco, stale sweat, stale dust, and stale horse. He wished longingly for a cold drink, a drink with ice in it, and he grinned at the thought. How long had it been since he had such a drink? Two years? Nearly three.

Yet this was a brand of warfare at which he felt at home. He had never been a spit-and-polish soldier, and never cared for the brass-bound posts back East. When he arrived on the southwest frontier he knew he had found a home . . . this was for him.

Lieutenant McDonald knew his Indians and they knew him, and every day he learned from them. He was a fighting man with no taste for formal drill, dress uniforms, or parade formations. Most drill was a waste of time, based on the demands of an outmoded idea of warfare, and their practical utility had ceased long since.

The only sensible training for troops was to teach them to fight and survive fighting, and every moment such training was not being given was a moment wasted.

It was battle that paid off, battle was the beginning and the end of a soldier's life. The Apache, the greatest guerrilla fighter the world ever knew, had never heard of close-order drill or any kind of training except in fighting and surviving.

Now, with four scouts ranging out ahead of them to cut any possible trail, they started on.

Yuma Bill rode ahead to join them, and before they had gone fifty yards, he turned in the saddle and waved.

The trail was there. A small party of Apaches, their trail not twelve hours old, moving toward the Gila. At once he sent a scout to inform Colonel Forsyth, then proceeded at a more cautious pace.

Within the mile another party of Indians had joined the first, making a band considerably larger than McDonald's detachment.

McDonald rode warily. He could sense the worry among the members of his command, and he did not blame them. He paused frequently to study the terrain, and changed his direction of travel several times to make ambush difficult.

He could *feel* Indians. Even Yuma Bill, ordinarily a tough, unresponsive sort, seemed nervous. Nobody but a fool would want to ride into an ambush of twice their number of Apaches, and it was their very wariness that saved them.

At this time McDonald was sixteen miles from the main body under Forsyth.

Somewhere in this vast sweep of desert and mountains was a small party of men and women with no experience at Indian fighting, and that party, if not already destroyed, was undoubtedly being stalked by the Apaches.

Heat waves lifted with the stifling dust. McDonald

mopped sweat and dust from his gaunt features and swore. His uniform felt stiff and heavy in the burning heat and his suspenders chafed his shoulders. The heat that rose from the sand and rocks was like that from the top of a stove.

Nothing moved . . . before them Horseshoe Canyon opened a way into the mountains. McDonald looked with misgiving at the towering cliffs, at the opening before them.

Yuma Bill, now riding point, was well out in front. He walked his horse into the rocky maw of the canyon. A moment later, McDonald saw him lift a hand.

When they came up to where he had stopped he was standing over the remains of a hastily smothered fire from which a thin tendril of smoke still lifted.

McDonald mopped the sweat from his face, squinting his eyes against the glare to survey the cliffs and the rocks. Deep within him he knew he was in serious trouble, for this fire could have been smothered only moments before . . . perhaps even as they approached.

Had the Apaches fled? Or did they lurk back in the rocks? And how many were there?

"How many would you guess?"

Yuma Bill shrugged. "Maybe five, maybe six here"— he gestured toward the rocks—"but who knows how many there?"

Should he now await Forsyth's arrival? Or should he advance into the canyon?

It was the problem of command, and no one could share his decision or his responsibility. If he sent another man for Forsyth and there were only a few Indians who had fled at his approach, Forsyth and the Fourth Cavalry would have ridden sixteen miles in the hot sun to no purpose. On the other hand, if he went ahead on his own, if he explored the situation a little further . . . ?

"We will move along," he said, but as he turned in his saddle to give the command there was a shadow of movement among the rocks. His shout was lost in a smashing volley, and two of his men tumbled from their saddles. One of them started up, lifting his rifle, only to fall again.

McDonald fired his pistol at a fleeting brown body and saw the Apache catch in midstride, then half-lunge, half-fall into the rocks and out of sight.

The roar of guns and the wild, shrill yells of the Indians were all about him. Coolly, he directed the movement of his small detachment to the crest of a low hill. Even as he shouted his orders he was aiming and firing, trying to make every shot count. This was the virtue of training, of conditioning, that in an emergency one always knew what to do. Panic only entered the empty mind.

Grabbing the shoulder of a scout, he swung the man toward his own horse. "Get Forsyth," he yelled hoarsely, amid the bark of guns.

The Indian leaped to the back of the horse and was gone in a long leap. That was the battalion racehorse and, if he had speed, now was the time to use it.

McDonald returned to directing the fight. He had but six unwounded men. Another had just fallen, and Yuma Bill, that invaluable man, had gone down after apparently getting off scot-free.

The Apaches were coming down among the rocks, closing in. The red-faced corporal, one of the best shots in the battalion, had dropped to one knee and was firing methodically as if on a rifle range.

Quickly as the attack began, it broke off. Four of his men gone, he awaited the next attack. They were in a nest of boulders atop the hill, and without any word from him the men went about making their position more secure.

Piling loose stones into gaps among the rocks, digging out the sand here, making a better firing position elsewhere. They had a little water, ammunition enough for a good fight, and a fair field of fire.

"Take your time," the lieutenant said. "Let's make them buy it."

An arm showed and a scout fired. Lieutenant McDonald believed it was a hit.

Two of the fleeing scouts had caught up ammunition pouches from the fallen men, and another had recovered a rifle. They had two extra weapons, which increased their immediate firepower.

Sixteen miles to go and sixteen to return, a brutal ride in horse-killing heat. Squatted on his heels behind a boulder, Lieutenant McDonald was glad it was Colonel Forsyth out there, for the colonel's memory of the Beecher Island fight would be fresh in his mind and he would understand the situation as only one can who has lived through it.

Riding with him would be four hundred veteran Indian fighters who would understand it, too.

The hilltop was an oven. McDonald shifted his grip on the gun long enough to dry his palm on his pants. "They'll be coming soon," he said. "Let's leave a couple of them on the sand."

Somewhere out upon the hot, dusty desert to the north and east a rider was killing a good horse getting to Colonel Forsyth and the Fourth Cavalry.

The Apaches came again, and again the Cavalry detachment broke the attack, with no casualties on either side. The Yuma scout beside Lieutenant McDonald was gasping from the heat as he fumbled cartridges into his pistol.

It was going to be a long afternoon.

THE SOUND OF distant firing came to the ears of Shalako Carlin. He drew up, listening.

That would be the Army and Chato. He sat his horse near the crest of the divide where Wolf Canyon started down the mountain to meet the Double Adobe Trail, considering the situation and weighing it against their own chances.

Chato had gone north with roughly forty Indians, some of whom had turned off for the attack on the hunting party. The rest had continued on to meet with the restless young warriors at San Carlos, but by now all the bodies should have joined forces, which would add up to nearly eighty Indians. It must be that force or a part of it now in battle off somewhere toward Stein's Peak.

The Apaches would make a fight of it, but if the Army was out in force they would pull out of the fight and run for the border. Whenever possible they would travel the high routes, and that meant they might easily take the Double Adobe Trail down which he now rode. They would be striking at anything they could hit and they would want horses.

The Army would be behind them. Hence, what remained for the hunting party was a fierce and desperate fight until the Army caught up with the Indians.

How much chance would the hunting party have against eighty Indians?

Seated astride his horse in the shade of a boulder, the roan close behind him, Shalako tried to view the situation as it would appear to one of the high-circling buzzards. That buzzard would see a wide skein of trails that were slowly being drawn tighter and tighter, and the center of the skein was held by the hunting party.

Four women, seven men active, and an eighth wounded. Well-armed, however, with ammunition enough for a reasonably long fight. Water, and a fairly good position to defend, but short of food.

There was a chance the Apaches might retreat down the valley, bypassing the mountains and the hunting party.

However, two of the men, Dagget and Mako, the cook, knew nothing of fighting, and the two who were good fighting men had never fought Indians. If they lasted thirty minutes against an all-out Apache attack they would be playing in luck.

"We don't have a chance," Shalako said aloud, "not a Chinaman's chance."

A bee buzzed idly in the brush alongside the trail, and the stallion stamped impatiently, wondering at the delay, but Shalako waited, building a smoke while he studied the terrain.

Off on his right lay Animas Valley, and a considerable plume of dust that indicated a fast-traveling party of horsemen, riding southwest by west and away from him. The Army, more than likely, for Apaches did not like to raise dust and usually scattered out to keep down the dust and so give less indication of their direction of travel.

The trail he followed was rarely used. It had been first

used, perhaps, when the mysterious Mimbres people lived in the area, perhaps even earlier. A white man traveling usually keeps to low ground, but an Indian or other primitive man keeps to the high country.

Shalako rode cautiously along the dim trail. The peaks around him rose eight to fifteen hundred feet above him. It was a rugged, lonely country where gnarled cedars clung to the raw lips of canyons and each cliff was banked by the shattered rock remaining from the ruin of itself.

A roadrunner poised on a rock beside the trail, flicking his long tail in a challenge to race, despite the heat. The roadrunner took off, gliding a few yards, then running on swift feet along the trail.

When Shalako had nearly reached the turnoff for the Park hideout, he went off the trail and into the rocks. Taking his Winchester, he left the horses in the shade and mounted the rocks, careful to give himself a background where he would not be outlined against the sky.

He could see almost two miles along the trail ahead from the vantage point he had chosen, and he was no more than two miles from the hideout itself. He had paused here for two reasons. He wanted to approach the camp at sundown, and he wanted to see if he was followed, and if anyone came along the trail.

He had seen no tracks. From all appearances that trail had not been used in months, perhaps not for years.

Moreover, the trail from here toward the hideout was, for the first mile, relatively exposed. He did not want to enter that trail until he was quite sure he would not be seen.

It was very hot. Overhead the inevitable buzzard soared with that timeless patience that comes from knowing that sooner or later all things that live in the desert become food for buzzards, and they had only to wait.

A tiny lizard raced on tiptoe across a hot rock and paused in the shade, tail up, its little throat pulsing as it gasped for air. After a moment the tail relaxed, the lizard quieted, and Shalako made no move.

He was tired and the sun was warm. Slowly, because a sudden move attracts attention, he turned his head and looked down at the horses. Both were browsing absently at the brush.

A dust devil danced in the trail below, then lost itself among the rocks. The lizard's lower lids crept drowsily over its eyes. Just a minute or two more, Shalako decided, and he would move along. The mountains were still, and they might be empty. His head lowered, and he settled to a more comfortable position. His head lowered again, bobbed, as he half-awakened, and then his eyes came all the way open.

There was a rider in the trail below, a rider wearing a wide hat and riding a sorrel horse. And he recognized the mount. It was Damper, one of Irina Carnarvon's mares.

He studied the rider, trying to place him, and then he remembered the black vest. It was Bosky Fulton, the man who had accompanied Rio Hockett. Shalako knew him.

The Arab's head was up, and he was scenting the wind.

"It's all right, Mohammet," Shalako said softly. "Everything is all right."

Shalako watched the rider. When he reached the fork of the trail, what would he do? And where were the others? Where was Hockett and the stolen wagon?

Suddenly the rider below drew up sharply, and seemed to be listening. Shalako listened also, and distinctly heard the sound of pounding hoofs. Fulton crossed the trail swiftly and went into the rocks, shucking his rifle as he did so.

Suddenly, around the bend of the trail came a riderless horse, a saddled horse with stirrups flapping.

It was Tally, Irina Carnarvon's other mare. The mare slowed, sniffed at the dust like a hound, and then came on. Many times Shalako had seen wild horses follow a trail like that, and follow it as skillfully as any wolf, and Tally was obviously following the trail of Damper.

Shalako's expression changed. Suppose the Apaches had had the mare? Suppose they were following her now?

It would be like an Apache to let the mare loose and follow her back to the other horses.

Tally paused in the trail and Shalako could see from his position how Fulton watched the mare, suspicious of her arrival, unaware that the horse he now rode and Tally had grown up together.

Suddenly Tally turned her head and lifted her nose to the wind. Despite the distance he could almost see her nostrils flare and, with a shock, Shalako realized the mare had caught the scent of the stallion! Even as he realized it, Tally turned from the trail and started up through the rocks toward him.

Fulton half-rose from his position, surprised by the mare's action. Undoubtedly Tally assumed that Damper would be where the stallion was, and was finding a way up through the maze of boulders.

Hurriedly, Shalako left his observation post and, returning to the stallion, he stepped into the saddle. Leading the roan, he started away, keeping the pyramid of rocks between himself and Fulton, and keeping to soft ground wherever possible. Behind him he could hear the mare, and he swore softly.

There was nothing for it now but to ride on to camp and hope that no Apache was trailing the mare.

Would Fulton add things up and come looking? It was doubtful. This was no time to be wasting around in the mountains, and Fulton undoubtedly had places he wanted to go . . . and judging by the direction he was headed he was going no farther than the nearest lot of Apaches.

When he had ridden a couple of hundred yards he concealed himself in the brush and waited for the mare to catch up. Mohammet could see her coming and started to whinny, but Shalako talked him out of it.

Watching beyond her, he saw she was not followed. Unless Fulton was a complete fool he would hole up somewhere and wait out the raid.

After a while, he continued on, and had gone scarcely half a mile when he saw Indian sign. It was a portion of the track of an unshod pony, and made that very morning. He waited, studying the terrain again. To a man who had seen an Apache wrapped in a dusty blanket appear as another boulder among the many lying about, there was no question of taking anything for granted.

Once, Shalako recalled, he had seen an Apache stand upright among a scattering of yucca trees, a few clusters of yucca blades stuck to his blanket, while an entire Army command rode past without seeing him.

Now, scouting the area with care, he found where two horses had been tied to a clump of brush. He found where the horses had cropped leaves from the brush, and, studying the branch ends to determine their freshness, he decided that the Apaches, riding unshod ponies and not captured stock, had been drawn to the hideout, probably by the smell of smoke, sometime during the previous night.

Studying the droppings left by the two horses to see what they had been eating, he saw the remains of plants that only grew well below the border. These two then were not part of the main band, but had probably followed Chato up from Mexico, leaving well after he had, and coming to this point by a long, hard ride.

They might have gone on to join Chato, perhaps to lead him back to this place. Nevertheless, they might still be lurking in the vicinity.

For some time, he scouted on foot, always keeping his horses in sight, for he well knew what an Indian could do when it came to stealing horses. More than once he had seen them stolen right from under a watcher's eyes. Yet he wished to know if they still remained nearby, and if others had been here.

Evening was near. Shadows grew longer at this hour, and the world became more quiet. The slightest sound traveled easily in the clear air of the desert and the mountains. This was the land of the sky . . . to know the sky, to feel the sky, to appreciate the sky one must be alone with it, somewhere along the hard-boned ridges or peaks at any time during the hours of light.

With darkness a change comes and distance is lost. The night brings all things near, although the desert by night is haunted by specters, with the silent standing columns of the cacti, the close-to-the-earth desert shrubs, or the black mystery of the mountains.

The desert and the sky both demand aloneness . . . to

know them completely one must be alone with them in the midst of their emptiness.

At such a time the body grows still, the mind becomes empty, a vast reservoir for the receiving of impressions. The slightest sound is heard or felt. Around one at such a time the desert spreads in all its mystery and strangeness, its timelessness, and overhead the sky is enormous.

The desert, too, seems to be listening, expecting.

Shalako waited and listened. And after a while he made his way back to the horses. The moccasins made moving with stillness a simple thing. No wild animal will break a twig or branch, nor will an Indian. Even in darkness he can sense the branch under his foot before his weight comes upon it, and places it elsewhere. This is one of the advantages of the moccasin.

Mounting up, he started along a bald ridge, keeping off the skyline, working his way toward the hideout. He had tied Tally's reins to the roan, so the horses could follow close behind him.

After a moment he saw the thin column of blue smoke mounting like an offering to the still evening sky. He was very wary now, not wanting to be shot by some trigger-happy member of the hunting party. When he had located the position guarded by Buffalo Harris, he called to him, knowing he would never fire a blind shot.

"All right," Harris replied conversationally, "come on in."

Shalako walked his horse along a cedar-clad slope and into the corner where Buffalo waited.

"Man, am I glad to see you!" Buffalo said. "I feel like a lone shepherd dog with a flock of sheep and the wolves closin' in."

"You got some coffee?"

"Coffee's all we do have. You got most of the grub."

"The Army's out." Shalako indicated the Springfield in the saddle boot. "Some good soldier died before he gave that up."

"Injun?"

"Uh-huh. Sneaked up on me last night. He was making a try for my horses."

"Kreuger's still alive. I don't see how he does it."

Irina was standing by the fire and her whole face lit up when she saw the mare. "Oh! You found Tally!"

"She found me." He did not tell her about Damper. There was time enough for that.

While Buffalo stripped the packs from the roan, Irina got him a blackened cup with coffee, and he brought them briefly up to date. He could tell them nothing except that the Army was in the field, that there was fighting to the northwest, which they already knew, and that within a matter of hours they might be in the path of the fleeing Apaches.

At the end he mentioned Bosky Fulton.

"He was alone?" Buffalo asked quickly.

"Are you making the guess I did?"

"That the rest of them were wiped out? I'd say that's a mighty good guess, unless he had trouble and cut loose from them, and Fulton wouldn't be likely to do that unless they came up with more than his share of the loot."

As he talked and drank coffee, he surveyed the situation. They had done pretty well, yet the area they were trying to defend was too large, there was too much chance of infiltration.

"If the Army is to the northwest"—von Hallstatt had come up to the fire—"why don't we move out and join them? After all, we have three horses now, and we should be able to move faster."

"The Army has its own troubles. You got in here on your own and you'd better figure to get out that way. Anyway, if you start for the Army you'll run head-on into Chato. He'll be coming this way on the run."

"That's supposition."

"Right. And if you want to figure it any other way, you go ahead."

"You would come with us if we started, would you not?" Julia asked.

"I would not."

"You are not very gallant."

"No, ma'am, I'm not. Neither is a bullet." He got to his feet. "You folks do what you want. If you want to make a stand here, I'm with you, but if you pull out you pull out on your own."

"You'd stay here alone?"

"Why not? To track a man even an Apache has to find tracks. I'd just stay right still and make no tracks at all. I'd go hungry four or five days if necessary, but I'd stay right here and sit it out."

He threw the dregs of his coffee into the fire and placed the cup on a rock, then he walked away to see to the horses.

Buffalo returned to his post and, after a little while, von Hallstatt did also.

The feed within the circle was almost gone, yet the horses could survive for a couple of days longer. And there was water.

Little enough had been done to strengthen the position, but it was just as well. What they must do now was pull back. The fire stood on low ground, in a sort of shallow basin, and no flames would be visible away from the circle of cedars, boulders, and brush that rimmed it.

The perimeter of defense was outside that circle, and should be drawn back. The cliff trail could be held by one man, and otherwise they seemed to have a good field of fire, and the best thing might be to make the first defense from the outer line, then fall back to the inner circle, for their force was too small.

He rubbed Mohammet down with a handful of sage, cleaned a few burrs from his tail, then did the same for Tally. He checked their shoes with care, then went to work on the roan. The mustang was in fine shape again, and nipped at his sleeve to prove it.

Irina joined him.

He was very conscious of her presence, but said nothing, working swiftly and silently. A little light remained in the sky, although the first stars had appeared.

"Mohammet likes you," she said, watching the Arab nuzzling him, "and he does not like many people."

"He's a good horse. He takes to this country like he was born to it."

"What are they like? The Apaches, I mean. Are they terribly savage?"

"Depends on how you look at it. Folks back East try to attribute Christian virtues and principles to the noble red man. They're wrong as can be. The red man is noble enough but his principles and way of life are completely different from ours.

"You can't say a man is good or bad because he thinks or doesn't think like you. They respect members of the tribe for altogether different reasons. The best thief among them is the one they admire most, and a killing from ambush is more to be desired than one in open combat.

"The best thief is the one who will be able to give most to his family, so all the Indian girls want a good thief for a husband. Stealing horses and fighting are not only their means to live, but their greatest pleasure. And they have none of our feeling about torture. Theirs is a hard, cruel life and men are valued for their courage, so they torture a man to see if he is brave, and also for fun.

"When they mutilate a body, sometimes it is from hatred or contempt, but just as often it is to cripple him so he won't be able to attack them if they meet in the afterlife."

"I had never thought much about such things, but I remember Father telling me about some of the customs of the people in Africa."

"Each tribe is different, but the Apaches were always fighters. But that's true of their kind everywhere. All the predatory peoples came from lands of sparse, unfertile soil, and their only wealth came from raiding and looting. The Vikings, the Prussians, the Mongols, the corsairs of Brittany . . . all of them made piracy and warfare a way of life, and it is the same with the Apache.

"You can't buy his friendship. If you are friendly he will believe it is because you are weak, and afraid of him. He may watch you for many days before he decides to attack, and he will never attack a party stronger than his own. He has none of our feeling about attacking a weaker or helpless enemy, and he respects only strength and courage."

"You are a puzzling man, Mr. Carlin. I wonder who you really are?" She searched his face, but his features showed nothing, nothing at all. "Who were you before you became Shalako?"

He straightened up, arching his back against the kink

from bending. "Don't get any foolish notions. I am not a cashiered Army officer, nor a foreign nobleman, nor a man escaping from a busted heart. The fact is, I'm a saddle tramp."

"I do not believe that."

"Your privilege."

"What do you want to *do*, Mr. Carlin? What do you want to *be*?"

"What I am. Did you ever top out on a ridge in wild country and look off across miles where nobody had ever been before? Did you ever ride for a month across country without ever seeing another human being? Or even the track of one? I have . . . and I want to again."

"And women? Have you never been in love, Mr. Carlin?"

"Sure, who hasn't? Matter of fact, I'm in love right now."

"Now?" She was startled . . . and dismayed.

"Sure . . . I'm in love with the smell of woodsmoke from that campfire over there, with the wind in the far-off pines, even with those Apaches out there."

"The Apaches? In love with *them*?"

"Sure . . . because they make me know I'm alive and if I slack off one second in their country they'll lift my hair. Say what you want about them, they are first-class fighting men."

The firelight flickered on the flanks of the horses. Somewhere in the outer darkness a pinecone dropped, but nothing else moved. She was very conscious of his nearness, but there was something exasperatingly elusive about him. He was beside her, and yet somehow he would fit into no category, no easy explanation, and he worried her, disturbed her deeply.

Her own exasperation led her on. "And have you no desire for a home? A family of your own?"

He listened into the darkness for a moment before replying. It was too quiet.

"Maybe . . . with the right woman. Or women."

"*Women?*"

"Sure," he said, straight-faced, "there's no reason why a good provider shouldn't have two, three, maybe even four women. Seems almost indecent, a man shutting other women out of his life like that. You never saw a rooster with only one hen, did you?"

"That's different!" She glanced at him quickly. "You're joking, of course."

"Now why would I joke? I've known several Indians who had more than one squaw, and they all seemed perfectly content. Makes it easier on them. They share the work, and there's always somebody to talk to."

He took up his rifle. "Better get some sleep. There may not be another chance."

Shalako strolled away, and she stared after him for a moment, then laughed. As he walked away, he smiled a little. She was quite a woman, too good a woman to be wasted on von Hallstatt.

He scouted from post to post, checking the positions of the defenders. When he reached von Hallstatt the German commented, "It is quiet out there."

"Too quiet. We will get an attack about daybreak."

"I hear nothing. I think there is nothing out there."

"Just watch yourself. If you slack off you will never live to see morning."

Shalako was distinctly uneasy, and he shifted his position, squatting on his heels beside von Hallstatt. "It's too damned quiet," he said after a moment, "I don't like the feel of it."

"Yes," von Hallstatt admitted, "there is something in the air. I feel it, too."

Shalako returned to the fire and his blankets. He spread them back at one edge, out of the firelight, and was asleep almost instantly.

Long since he had learned to sleep in snatches, and to catch a bit of sleep whenever possible. He had been asleep a little over two hours when he suddenly awakened. It was still dark, yet day could not be far away. He went to the trickle of water that ran away from the spring and dipped his fingers into the clear, cold water, splashing his face with it and combing his hair with his fingers. Then he put on his hat and walked to the fire.

Henri was there, his face drawn with weariness, nursing a cup of black coffee.

Shalako filled his own cup and squatted on his heels. "They'll be coming just before sunup . . . with the first light."

Henri nodded. "How many do you think?"

"Anybody's guess. Six or seven can be as dangerous as twice that many. They have more cover here than they had down below."

One by one the men who had slept moved into position. Mako returned to watch the cliff trail, Dagget took a position where he could look down into and along both sides of Elephant Butte Canyon. Roy Harding was to cover the area between Park Canyon and the edge of the cliff they had mounted. Henri covered the head of Park Canyon itself.

"Buffalo," Shalako said, "you, von Hallstatt, and I

will cover the trail and the area between the two canyons."

Von Hallstatt had returned to the fire for the planning. Now he put his pipe between his teeth and glanced quizzically at Shalako. He indicated the peak that reared up nearly four hundred feet behind them, Elephant Butte itself.

"What about that? A good rifleman up there could make our position untenable."

"We've got to gamble. Their only way up there is from the canyon side, a much steeper cliff than here, and we don't have a man to put up there."

It was still dark, but as they moved into position the isolated trees and boulders were beginning to stand out. High in the heavens overhead there was a faint tinge of pink on a cloud, nothing more.

The coolness of night lay upon the land. Nothing stirred. Shalako settled into position, studying the terrain before him. He swept it with a quick, searching glance, then starting far out at the limit of his range of vision, he searched the ground methodically in side-to-side sweeps until close in to his position.

Each rock, each tree, each shrub he studied with particular care, making allowances for the growing light, studying the contours, the length of the shadows.

The first shot was unexpected and it came from Harding's position. A second shot followed the first, and then a shadow stirred in front of his position, but before he could bring his rifle to bear, it was gone.

He waited, his rifle ready, but there was no further movement, and no sound.

Now the Apaches knew they were prepared. Was this

an actual attack? Or was it merely a few exploratory advances?

There was a stir of movement beside him, and Irina moved up into position, rifle in hand.

"This is no place for you," he whispered.

She settled into position. "Why not? I can shoot, can't I?"

It was full light, but the sun was not yet above the horizon. There was no movement, no shooting from anywhere. The very silence worried him, for the Apaches must know their weakness . . . and they also knew about the women.

Several times he thought he heard distant rifle fire, but he could not be sure.

Shalako shifted his rifle in his hands and started to speak, then broke off sharply.

From off on their right there was a faint cry, then a shot.

Henri leaped up and suddenly dashed forward and, dropping into a new position, he fired almost as he touched the ground.

And then the cry came again. It was from Roy Harding, and he was hurt.

Shalako left the ground running. A bullet spat gravel just ahead of him as he made a rolling dive for shelter behind some rocks, another bullet splintering rock fragments as he landed safely.

Rolling over, he came up running, then dove for shelter again just within sight of Harding.

The teamster was crawling back, dragging a bloody leg behind him, but even as Shalako sighted him, an Apache lunged from the brush, knife in hand.

Rolling to a sitting position, Shalako fired without

bringing the rifle to his shoulder, and the bullet stopped the leaping Indian in midair. A hoarse scream tore the Apache's throat, but he fell near Harding, slapping and stabbing wildly with his knife.

Harding kicked out with his good leg and his heel caught the Indian full in the face. Blood splattered from a broken nose, but despite the bullet and the kick the Apache reared up to his knees and threw himself at Harding.

Harding caught the Indian's knife wrist and wrenched the arm back, falling atop the Indian. There was a moment of brief, fierce struggle on the bloody gravel, and then Harding fell away as Shalako reached his side.

Harding's leg had been torn wickedly by a ricocheting bullet, and he had lost a lot of blood.

Swiftly, Shalako gathered him up, crouched, then left the ground in a plunging, staggering run. A bullet *whapped* the air close to his ear, and then he was out of range and down in the hollow where the fire was.

Gently, he put the young teamster down. "Take care of him, Laura," he said, and ducked back to the firing line.

Picking his rifle from the ground where he had left it in going after Harding, he dropped flat and peered out between the rocks.

He was gasping from his exertions and when he glimpsed an Apache he fired . . . and missed.

Desperately he tried to steady his breathing, but nothing showed except for dancing heat waves. The coolness of the morning had fled. Suddenly he heard the sound of horses' hoofs. They were coming, the rest of the Indians were coming.

Far below on the trail, a good five hundred yards off, he saw a rider pass, an Apache.

He sighted at the gap between the rocks. Maybe . . . just maybe. He took a careful sight, gathered some slack on the trigger, and waited. Carefully, he took in a breath and let it slowly out, and then a horse's head came into sight and he squeezed off his shot.

Even as the rifle leaped in his hands, the rider came into his sights, then vanished. The report of the shot racketed among the rocks.

He drew back and mopped the sweat from his brow to keep the salt from blinding him. He fed another shell into his Winchester, and waited.

It was time to draw back. They were too spread out and if the Apaches ever got behind them they would have no chance, none whatever.

A slight whisper of sound reached him, and listening he heard it no more, yet he knew that sound. It was the rubbing of coarse cloth on rock.

The canyon . . .

With infinite care he inched along on his belly to a position where he could look into the canyon. It was no more than sixty feet deep at that point, and he could see three Apaches working their way up the steep side.

He was starting to lift the rifle when he noticed the wedge of rock. It was a huge, piano-sized rock poised on the lip of the canyon.

Working his way over to it, he put his back against another rock, doubled his knees back almost to his chest, and put his moccasined feet against the wedge of rock. The rock teetered, but did not fall.

Carefully, he teetered it once again, and when it started to teeter forward, he shoved with all his strength. The stone leaned far out, and then toppled over. From below there came a hoarse scream, ending in the tremendous crash of the falling boulder, then the rattle of pursuing rocks.

Taking up his rifle he worked his way along the line of defense, calling them all back. Henri had a cut over his eye caused by a flying rock splinter, but there were no other injuries.

Once more they took up their positions, but this time at the edge of the circle that surrounded the campfire and backed up against the cliff wall and the tower of Elephant Butte.

Hans Kreuger was still alive, still silent, rarely asking for attention, offering no evidence of the pain he was feeling. Harding was weak from loss of blood, but his leg had been bandaged.

"If we only knew what was happening!" Laura exclaimed. "If we only knew whether the Army was coming or not."

"They may not even know we exist," Dagget said.

"They will know," Buffalo replied. "By now they know. They may have cut our trail somewhere, and they will know."

He returned to his new position, and settled down for a long wait. He could hear the murmur of voices around the fire, occasionally see them moving there, although he was well back among the rocks and trees. One thing he knew: When this was over he was quitting. He was going to get a stake and a ranch somewhere away from Indians . . . in some safe, sane, reasonable country.

He had been there for some time when he began to feel uneasy. He shifted his position, studied all the terrain about him, but nothing had changed.

Far off, softened by distance, he heard the hammer of gunfire. Somebody was having one hell of a fight. Maybe if the Army gave Chato a whipping he would be running so fast there would be no time to stop.

He yawned and shifted his position. Suddenly his breath stilled. That rock out there, no larger than a man's fist . . . was turned over.

Now the heavy side of a rock is always down in a place where wind and water can reach it, so something had passed that way, moving very fast, and had inadvertently overturned the rock. Something coming toward *him*!

And there was nothing . . .

Really worried now, he got to his feet and checked the area again. Could he have overlooked that rock when he took the position first? He was a man who always noticed such things for such things were his life. But could he, this time at least, have made a mistake?

It was very quiet.

He should move away. This place had good cover and he was well hidden, but nevertheless, he should move. If something was that close to him . . . ?

But nothing was there.

He listened, and heard no sound. He studied again every tree, every rock. He dropped back to his knees finally, and put his Winchester on the ground. He reached back to shift his knife into a better position, and when he did a rock that was not a rock moved behind him, a muscular forearm slid around his neck and across his throat. He was jerked cruelly back, his breath shut off, and he was fighting with his hands to tear the enclosing arm free when the knife went into his ribs.

His big body heaved powerfully, and he almost broke free, and then the knife slid between his ribs again, and then again. Slowly his muscles relaxed and the idea of the ranch was gone from his mind, the idea of survival was gone, and then life was gone. In that big body, so filled with strength and energy and that mind with plans . . . there was nothing, nothing at all.

A brown hand reached over and took up his rifle, unbuckled his cartridge belt, took his tobacco and pistol.

Tats-ah-das-ay-go slid back among the rocks, crossed a narrow space and crouched in the brush where his brown body merged easily with the sandstone and lava.

When he moved again he was well back in the rocks on the rim of Elephant Butte Canyon where he could watch the camp. *Tats-ah-das-ay-go* was a patient man. He had killed once and safely, soon he would kill again, but he was in no hurry. These people weren't going anywhere.

He had already chosen his next victim.

On that hot afternoon of April 23, Lieutenant Colonel Sandy Forsyth was seated on a low knoll studying the terrain about him. There had been no word from Lieutenant Hall, but that worried him less than the fact that he had not heard from Lieutenant McDonald, who had a mere handful of scouts.

His glasses swept the country, caught a flicker of movement, and reversed their field.

A rider . . . coming like hell after him.

His glasses brought the rider closer. An Indian by the way he rode . . . *Jumping Jack!*

That horse was Jumping Jack, McDonald's mount, and the company racehorse, the fastest horse in the regiment.

Trouble . . .

The colonel moved the command down the slope on

a course to intercept the rider, and then drew up to await the man as he came nearer.

The Mohave scout leaped to the ground as the horse broke under him and rolled over on the hot sand. The message was quick, concise, definite. McDonald was under heavy attack by a large force. Three or four of his men had been killed.

It was sixteen miles of riding in blistering hot country. It might kill every horse in the command but there was no choice. There had been another time, away back, when Sandy Forsyth had waited, stretched out on his back in the grass of Beecher's Island, suffering from an ugly wound, and praying for relief.

———

ATOP THE KNOLL where Lieutenant McDonald was making his fight, his canteen gave off only an empty sound. Two of his men were down, wounded and gasping under the broiling sun, for there was no shade.

Checking the loads on the three rifles he was now using, he glanced around at his small command. The red-faced corporal, redder of face now, was still willing and able. One of the Mohaves had a livid gash across his cheek from a bullet, and one of the wounded men was delirious and raving of mountain lakes, of shadows, and of fish splashing in the cool water. Occasionally he whimpered with an almost animal sound. The other wounded man had dragged himself to the rocks and was ready with his rifle.

The Apaches were confident. They moved forward in a short, quick dash. McDonald, a dead shot with a rifle, picked up the first weapon. An Apache moved and the lieutenant fired, then fired again, taking the Apache in midstride. The Indian fell, then scrambled to safety among the rocks.

Miles away, riding under the blazing sun, Forsyth heard the shots. He might be in time then . . . he might still be in time.

There were seventy-five Indians along the cliffs of Horseshoe Canyon who had taken no part in the attack on the patrol. They awaited bigger game. The trouble was, they did not expect the number that came.

Loco, who directed the fighting, put up a stubborn battle against superior forces and superior arms, fighting a wary rearguard action, and retreated slowly into the depths of the canyon.

It was not the sort of fighting to be relished by either side. Targets were few and elusive despite the number of men engaged, and there were not many bodies falling. Despite the number of deaths in combat there are never so many as one would expect from the amount of shooting done.

The Apache was always cautious in his fighting, and the soldiers had fought Apaches before and learned from them things no War Department manual could teach, so it was a careful, relentless struggle where every shot was meant to kill but targets were few. There were no amateurs in the battle of Horseshoe Canyon.

The battle lasted until darkness before the soldiers withdrew. They had driven the Indians into the rocks and into the night, and from there on no commander with an ounce of sense would risk his men.

Nor did Forsyth have any doubts that the Apaches were on the run. Detaching Captain Gordon and Lieutenant Gatewood to the pursuit, Forsyth turned to interrogating the prisoners. They had taken but two, one a wounded warrior, the other an ancient squaw. Neither admitted knowing of the hunting party, yet one of the dead Apaches carried a rifle on which was carved the name of Pete Wells.

"It doesn't mean they've been wiped out," McDonald decided, "only that they got Wells, or got his rifle somehow."

"Chato wasn't with this bunch. He must have found them. The rifle could have been carried by a messenger."

Night was upon them and they had no choice but to remain where they were. The brutal charge across the desert in the blazing sun had left the horses in no shape for further travel, so whatever was to be done must be done the following day.

"I wish," Forsyth said, "that we could hear from Hall."

———

HANS KREUGER DIED as the sun went down, going quietly. He asked for a drink of water and Laura brought it to him, and when he thanked her he put his head back on the doubled-up coat that was his pillow and looked up at the sky where the first stars had appeared. He did not move again, nor did he speak.

His passing brought deep depression to the group. Pete Wells had been killed, but he had not been well-known to any of them but Buffalo Harris, and he had been killed far from them. Kreuger was of their own group, and he had been a well-liked, quiet, and sincere young man.

Roy Harding lay wounded, their food supply was dwindling, and then Shalako Carlin found the body of Buffalo Harris.

The big hunter had been dead but a few minutes, and

the manner of his death was apparent, even in the gathering dusk. The slight smudges of toes digging into the sand, the indications of a brief, hopeless struggle were there. One thing was immediately apparent to Shalako—Buffalo Harris had been killed by no ordinary Apache.

The buffalo hunter had been familiar with all the tricks and devices of the Indian, and was a veteran of many a skirmish. Yet there had been slight struggle, and no sound. No wolf or mountain lion could have killed more swiftly, silently, and efficiently.

The killer could have taken the weapons and slipped back among his own people, but Shalako had an uneasy feeling this was not so. He might still be among them, waiting for the chance to kill again.

The world of the Apache was not a large one. From the Tucson area to somewhat east of El Paso, from deep in Sonora and the Sierra Madre to central New Mexico—they raided beyond that area, and the White Mountain Apaches were farther north—this land was theirs.

Within that area among the Apaches and those aware of them, there were names that worked magic. Names of men alive today, names of a few but recently dead. Mangas Colorado, Cochise, Nana, Geronimo, Victorio, Chato . . . and a dozen others. These were their warriors and their chieftains.

Among them also there were tales of other warriors, warriors who were not leaders. It was the name of one of these that came to Shalako's mind now.

The manner of the kill, the silence, the skill . . . it had all the earmarks.

The present area of their camp was no more than an acre. Except for that space immediately surrounding the fire, it consisted of brush, broken rock, deep gashes into the base rock along the lips of the canyons, scattered trees, and behind them, Elephant Butte.

Kreuger was dead, Harris was dead, and Harding was wounded. Only five men remained on their feet and able to fight, and there were the four women. Von Hallstatt and Henri were both good men, Dagget and Mako untried and inexperienced. He walked back to the fire.

"What is it, Shalako?" Irina was on her feet looking at him.

"Stay close to the fire," he said, "and stay together through the night. There's an Indian inside the circle."

"How could there be?" Julia demanded. "We've been watching."

"He killed Buffalo." Shalako turned back to Irina. "Let Julia take over the cooking. From now on I want you and Laura to stand guard with rifles. If you see an Indian, kill him."

"Suppose we hunt him down?" Henri suggested. "He hasn't much room in which to maneuver."

"It would be like going out in the night to feel around in the grass for a rattlesnake. You'd find him, all right."

Henri relieved Mako at the cliff's edge, and the cook returned to the fire.

Shalako prowled restlessly, then he, too, returned to the fire.

"That's *Tats-ah-das-ay-go* out there," he said. "I am sure of it."

"How can you be sure?" Mako asked.

"The way he killed, and the fact that he came into the camp area instead of leaving it."

"How can you be sure he did?"

"Call it a feeling. He's here, all right, and I'm sure that's who he is. He's a great warrior, perhaps the greatest in the Apache nation, and he's a lone wolf. Even the other Apaches are afraid of him. Stays to himself, usually travels alone. I'd say he was downright unsocial."

He had stalked bighorn sheep in the mountains and deer and antelope upon the low ground. He would understand the use of every shadow, every crevice, every bush. He would know how to hide where it seemed impossible anything could hide, and he would be more deadly than any rattler for he would offer no warning.

It was the waiting that worried them. It worried him, too, but Shalako was a patient man. These others were not patient. All of them, even von Hallstatt, were undisciplined. They wanted what they wanted without waiting. They had never learned to cope with time.

The West taught one how to cope with time, for time measured all things. One did not say it was so many miles from here to yonder, but it was so many days ride. Everything was measured by time and time measured everything.

"Why have you stayed?" Irina said.

"A lady loaned me a horse. Let's just say I was grateful."

"You needn't have been. To be perfectly honest I was worried about my horse. I couldn't bear the thought of his being eaten."

"It adds up to the same thing. Anyway, you could have come with me."

"And leave the others? You knew I would not do that."

He was following the conversation with only half his attention, the rest of it was out there in the rocks, trying to understand the thinking of an Indian who was planning to kill one or all of them.

She had been silent for several minutes, evidently thinking along the same lines, for she said, "How could you know who he is? The Indian, I mean."

"Every person identifies himself by his habits, his mannerisms. Sometimes you know them by the tracks they leave, sometimes by the tracks they do not leave. Little things add up to make a picture. . . ."

"Will knowing who he is help?"

"It might. It makes him easier to understand, and sometimes you can outguess a man you know."

Roy Harding overheard them. "Who did you say?"

"*Tats-ah-das-ay-go,* the Quick-Killer."

"I've heard of him."

Among the rocks the Apache heard his name spoken and was frightened. An Apache's name is a closely guarded secret in most cases, and to possess a man's name is to possess a power over him.

His eyes fixed apprehensively on the big man who had spoken his name. By what medicine had this man learned who he was?

This was the one he heard called Shalako. He was the man with whom the rains came.

Tats-ah-das-ay-go watched the big man closely. He was a man to be avoided . . . a great warrior . . . a man with whom the Apache would have risked anything to meet in battle. But Shalako knew his name . . . there was big medicine in this. Nobody had seen him, but Shalako spoke of him.

He remained where he was. The man on the cliff, he was to be the next one.

Shalako glanced around at those whom he could see, and the tension was obvious. Edna Dagget looked drawn and haggard, starting at the least sound, on the ragged edge of hysteria.

Julia Paige seemed all eyes. The dark circles beneath them indicating lack of sleep and worry. Count Henri had lost weight, but he was cool, competent, and ready.

"You'll have to watch, Roy," Shalako said. "Don't rely on the girls. They aren't up to it. Keep your gun handy . . . they may try to finish you off."

"I'm wondering what became of Bosky Fulton. You said you saw him out there, and there's been no shooting."

"Holed up. That's if he's smart. If he tried to run for it now he'd be sure to be killed."

Shalako knew that Forsyth would have his own problems. By the sound of the firing they had heard, a battle had taken place between two considerable forces. He could only surmise the results, but he imagined the Army would have won. On the other hand they might have suffered, might have lost horses, and either might slow them up.

He glanced around the circle. Their small supply of food would not go much further. The food would give out before the ammunition, and how disciplined were these people?

Could they hold out two days? Three?

Forsyth might be within a dozen miles of them now, but Forsyth could not know where they were. Tomorrow, if an attack was made, he might hear the gunfire. If he were in battle himself, he would not.

Yet by this time Forsyth's scouts would certainly have told him the hunting party had headed south . . . if they didn't leap to the conclusion that it had been wiped out or taken prisoner.

Laura Davis was the daughter of a United States Senator and by now the wire from Washington would be hot with demands that something be done.

Say three days longer. They must hold out three days longer.

There would surely be an attack tomorrow, which would mean that superstition or not, *Tats-ah-das-ay-go* would kill tonight. He was a lone warrior, and he would want to count coup again before the final attack.

Getting to his feet he circled the line of defense. By day each man could be seen from the central point where the fire was, but by night the positions of several of the men on guard were lost in darkness. It was these about whom he worried.

Von Hallstatt looked up as Shalako squatted beside him. "Don't remain in any position very long," Shalako warned. "Keep moving, watch the shadows. I think he will try to kill at least one more tonight."

Dagget was eager, rather than frightened. For the first time in his life he was actually in the field. He looked around at Shalako. "I'm a fool," he said. "But do you want to know something? I like this."

"It puts a man on edge, all right."

"It's living! Really living! I always wanted to be a soldier, but Father advised diplomacy and, of course, Edna would hear of nothing else. I never had a chance to even try it."

"You'll have to get some sleep. After a bit we will manage to sleep, two at a time."

"I don't mind. I'll stay here."

Henri was settled down with his back against a towering boulder. He had chosen a good, concealed and relatively protected position that offered a good field of fire. The position was so good that it was unlikely he would be attacked.

Shalako went back to the fire, which had been allowed to die down. The fuel they had close by must now be sufficient, for there was no possibility of leaving the circle for more.

Irina was near the fire, and Laura also. Julia Paige was lighting a cigarette for Harding, who lay stretched on a pallet just back from the edge of the firelight.

"It's getting cooler," Laura said. "I can never get used to how cool the nights become after such hot days."

"When I was a little girl in India," Irina commented, "I used to lie awake at night . . . the heat was stifling . . . and listen to the tigers out in the jungle. I could lie there and imagine them slinking through the jungle, their great black and gold bodies moving as soundlessly as a snake."

"We're all going to be killed," Edna Dagget said. "We're all going to be killed, and you just sit there, talking."

"Ain't much else to do," Harding said mildly. "Nobody's going out in that jungle after no Apache. Nobody in his right mind."

He glanced at Irina. "I'd sure admire to hear more about that tiger country, ma'am. I heard somebody say you'd hunted them with your pa."

"Yes, I did."

"Hunted mountain lions a few times," Harding said. "No fun to that, once you get the hang of it. Lion's a mighty mean animal, but they sure ain't got any brains. I've trapped two lions in the same trap on the same day . . . with the smell of lion and blood all over the place. You'd never do that with a wolf, nor most any other animal."

IRINA'S HANDS LAY in her lap. They were beautiful hands, but capable hands, too, the hands a woman should have.

It had been a long time since Shalako had thought of himself in connection with any woman as beautiful as Irina, and he was a fool to begin now. He had nothing to offer, and no doubt she would be astonished and then amused if she realized he had even thought of such a thing.

He was a saddle tramp, a drifter with a pistol and a Winchester, a man who rode wild country with wilder men, and to that he had best keep himself. He was Shalako, the man who brought the rains with him . . . and she was Lady Irina Carnarvon, daughter of an ancient Welsh-Irish family. Two people could not be farther apart . . . and the fact that for a few brief years he had known a life not unlike hers was of no importance, and all that was forgotten now. Or was it?

At best, those years had been an interlude, for he was a Western man, and only a Western man . . . nor did he wish to be anything else.

Shalako threw the dregs of his coffee into the fire. "I'm going out there," he said, "and find that Indian."

They looked at him as if he were mad, and perhaps he was, but, after all, this was the thing he did best, and why should he shrink from trying? He knew enough about that Apache out there to know that hunting a rattlesnake in the grass with your hands might be far safer than hunting that Indian at night among the rocks.

"If I don't find him," he said, "somebody will die before daylight."

"And what if something happens to you?" Irina asked. "What shall we do then?"

He looked at her with sudden bitterness. "You know how much of a hole a man leaves when he dies? The same hole you leave in the water when you pull your finger out. I'll leave no more than that, nor be missed more than an hour or two . . . If anybody here can find that Indian without having him find them first, it's me. I've got a chance."

"Don't go," Irina said.

"We could all come in close to the fire," Laura suggested, "and each could watch the others."

"And by daylight you'd be surrounded and helpless. No, I've got to try." He paused a moment, thinking of what lay out there.

Laura added a stick to the fire and the firelight that blazed up caught Harding's face. "Better wait," he said, "somebody's coming."

He was lying on the ground, and caught the sound before any of them. And then they could all hear it, the pounding of hoofs . . . a wild, shrill cry in the night, and the racing hoofs coming closer and closer.

Shalako sprang back from the fire and lifted his gun. They heard the sharp challenge from von Hallstatt, then a more distant shot, and then they heard a voice say, "Hold your fire, Fritz. I'm coming in."

And the rider came on into the circle and into the firelight. It was Bosky Fulton.

He slid from the saddle, grinning. It was a taunting grin, yet Shalako could see the wariness in it, the animal-like watchfulness.

"There's a passel of Indians out there an' come morning I figured you'd need help. And I ain't sayin' I wouldn't be glad of it my ownself."

Von Hallstatt came into the circle. "You damned thief," he said. "You damned, cheap, murdering thief."

Fulton turned on the German, but he kept smiling. "Now most any other time, Fritz, I'd kill you for that. Right now I figure we got plenty of killin' to do without us shootin' each other."

He squatted on his heels by the fire and picked up a cup. Coolly, he poured himself a cup of coffee. Then he looked up. "If there's one Indian out there, there's fifty. They done give the Army the slip, and that there Forsyth is chasing off toward the border after six or eight Apaches who are making tracks enough for fifty. The rest of them are bunched out here to take this outfit."

"But you came in to help us?" Laura said skeptically. "It doesn't sound like you."

"I came in to he'p myself," Fulton said, grinning insolently. "I'd no chance to catch the Army, and it was gettin' mighty lonesome out there by myself. I figured I better take a chance with you folks."

"You're a cheap coward," von Hallstatt said. "You ran like a rabbit once, and you'll do it again."

Bosky Fulton's lips tightened a little. The smile remained but it was stiff. "Now you'll die for that," he said. "If the Apaches don't kill you, I will."

"You have your nerve," Irina said.

"Sure." He looked at her with a flickering glance that did not quite remove his attention from von Hallstatt. "And if you want to keep General Fritz alive, ma'am, you better quiet him down. If he figures to talk to me like that, he should have that rifle in firing position before he opens his yap."

Fulton had not noticed Shalako, and now Shalako stepped down from the shadows near a tree where he had stepped at the rush of hoofs. "This is fool talk, Fulton, so if you want to stay here with us, cut it out."

Fulton's shoulders hunched as if from a blow. His yellow eyes clung to von Hallstatt. He desperately wished to turn, but he feared to turn his back on the German, and von Hallstatt, seeing his quandary, smiled at him.

"Now that takes a lot of guts," Fulton said. "Coming up behind a man like that. Suppose you meet me face to face."

Deliberately, Shalako stepped up behind him and took him by the shoulder and turned him sharply around. "All right, Fulton"—he stood within two feet of him—"I'm ready. Want to make something of it?"

Fulton stared at Shalako, and Shalako's cold eyes did not waver. "You can stay, Fulton, as long as you carry your weight. When you stop carrying it, or start trouble, out you go."

"And who'll make me?" Fulton was shaking with fury, but there was something in Shalako that worried him. Shalako was not worried, he was not afraid, he was even contemptuous.

"I'll make you, Fulton. You make trouble here and I'll run you out of camp, like a whipped dog. And when you decide to try gunning me, just go right ahead. I won't be drunk and I won't be scared, and even if you get a bullet into me, *I'll kill you*. Make up your mind to that, Fulton. *I'll kill you*."

Harding had lifted himself on an elbow. For the first time Fulton saw that Harding held a Colt in his hand.

"Bosky, you're a nervy man. *Tats-ah-das-ay-go* is out there in the rocks. Somebody's got to go after him. Why don't you show us just how tough you are and go get him?"

Fulton's anger and frustration mounted within him, yet through it all stabbed a clear, hard grain of sense. *Tats-ah-das-ay-go . . . good God!*

"He killed Buffalo a few hours ago, but he's inside the circle somewhere. He's in the rocks out there, not more than fifty yards away right now. Why don't you go get him?"

Bosky Fulton drew back, then shrugged. "Let him come to me. I ain't lost anything out there in those rocks."

He had taken a gamble, coming back here, but less of a gamble than it would have been out there among the Apaches.

Nor was he worried. If he could last out the Indian raids with this outfit, he would cut and run when it was over, and before they would ask too many questions about their jewelry and money. The thing to do was to get out before the Army found them.

As for von Hallstatt, that German needed killing and he was going to personally take care of that.

He remembered Shalako and was faintly uneasy. The feeling angered him, for there was nothing about Shalako that he should be worried about. Who was he, after all, but a drifting cowhand and prospector . . . although he had the look of a tough man.

A couple of .44 slugs would make him look a lot less tough.

———

WITH THE FIRST coming of day the defenders drew back so they could offer mutual support.

"Why did he have to come here?" Laura asked, indicating Fulton. "I hate that man. And he's absolutely filthy."

"He can shoot," Shalako replied. "We can use him."

"Nevertheless, I don't like him. He's mean, vicious, and cruel." For the first time Shalako learned that Fulton had planned to take the two girls with him when they left.

"A fool thing," he said. "In this country a man can get away with murder sometimes, and with stealing often enough, but a man who bothers a woman will get his neck stretched."

Shalako took up his Winchester and went over to where von Hallstatt had dug out the sand to make a better firing position. Shalako dropped down beside him and, squinting through the rocks, studied the field of fire. It was a good one.

"Watch yourself around Fulton," he said. "He means to kill you."

Von Hallstatt glanced sharply at him but, without returning the glance, Shalako continued. "He's a killer. He's killed a half-dozen men in gun battles, and likes to have the name of being a fast man with a gun. He's proud, and he's touchy. He needs us right now, and we can use him, but when this tapers off, you be ready. Never be without a gun, and never let him have an even break. He'll kill you."

"Can he shoot that fast and with accuracy?"

"You just bet he can."

"We will see. I do not like Herr Fulton."

Shalako got up to move. "Neither do I, but he's no fool, so be careful."

"Why do you warn me? I am not your friend."

Shalako grinned suddenly. "Nor am I yours, but this is

a matter of tactics, and his are different than yours. I figured you'd better know what to expect."

"You seem to think a good deal in terms of tactics."

"I want to live."

"Perhaps," von Hallstatt mused, "he will fight according to my tactics. He is a proud man, you say."

Shalako took up a position among the rocks. He glanced slowly around. Their circle was drawn back now, and was scarcely thirty yards from side to side. Close behind them loomed Elephant Butte, on their right, and right beside them, the lip of the canyon, and on the other side, just a short distance away, the cliffs.

"Irina"—Shalako motioned to her—"fill the canteens. You gather all our gear and take it to the edge of the canyon near the butte."

He paused . . . it was very still out there. The last of the stars were gone. There was a faint gray over the distant mountains to the east. "And get Harding back there."

Von Hallstatt was on his right, Dagget close on his left. Bosky Fulton was just beyond.

"Henri," he said, "you relieve Mako. Let him get something to eat."

The Frenchman left the fire and moved away toward the cliff's edge.

He was back almost at once. "Mako's dead," Henri said. "He's been stabbed."

There was a silence. Irina felt herself cold with horror. Another of them gone . . . how many more would go?

"He made a good omelet," Laura said. "He made the best omelet I ever ate."

"He would like nothing better than to hear you say that," Henri said. "He was proud of his work."

"You're not just a-foolin'?" Bosky asked, looking

from one to the other. "That damn' Apache killer is really here?"

"You watch yourself, Fulton," Harding taunted, "or he'll take your hair. That tangled mop of yours would make a pretty sight hanging from his bridle. I can close my eyes and just see it there."

"Shut up!" Bosky snarled over his shoulder.

They lapsed into silence. Another gone, and an attack was coming. It was coming and they all knew it was, but when it came it was not as they expected. It was a mounted attack and it came with a rush—about a dozen horsemen coming through the trees, fleeting, indefinite targets.

Von Hallstatt and Fulton fired as one man, and an Indian pony reared, throwing its rider. Dagget fired, killing the Indian as he started to mount.

"Did you see that?" Dagget yelled excitedly. "I got him!"

He had come halfway to his feet with excitement when a bullet burned his neck, and he dropped flat, clasping a hand to his bloody flesh, an expression of startled horror on his face.

The attack broke as suddenly as it had begun, with riderless horses disappearing among the trees. The Apaches had dropped to the ground close up, and now the small fort was ringed with enemies, all within an easy bowshot of their meager defenses.

From the edge of the cliff behind them they heard Henri fire, then fire again. The sound of his heavy rifle was easily distinguished from the others.

Dagget sat, his legs spread wide, dabbing at his bloody neck. "They damned near killed me!" he said, in a shocked tone.

"But they didn't. You're only scratched." Roy Harding was crawling toward them. "Let me up there."

"You had better return," von Hallstatt told the teamster. "Soon we retreat, and there is no time for carrying you back."

"He's right," Shalako agreed.

An Indian started up and Bosky Fulton fired. The Indian fell, and Bosky shot into him before he could more than make a move to rise.

An angry yell from the trees drew another shot from Fulton.

Count Henri fired again from the cliff, and from the rocks on the side of the Butte, Irina fired. She was shooting over their heads into the trees.

There was a lull. The sun mounted, the heat grew intense. Nothing stirred.

From time to time a bullet nipped at the rocks. The brilliant blue of the sky was gone and it seemed misted over . . . but there could be no mist in such a place. Von Hallstatt glanced at it inquiringly. "It is peculiar," he said. He started to fill his pipe and glanced at it again. "I think it is dust!"

The air grew suddenly cooler. Irina called to them from the rocks, and pointed. They turned to look and saw the horizon obscured with a far-off cloud.

Shalako turned quickly to von Hallstatt. "We've got to fall back and bunch up," he said. "That's a dust storm. Maybe a norther. I've seen the temperature drop thirty degrees in less than an hour in such a storm."

"Thirty degrees? It is too much!"

"Did you ever spend a spring in the Texas Panhandle? Or country adjoining it? My friend, you've seen nothing until you have!"

Quickly, they fell back. Bosky Fulton had already gone for the horses and, with Shalako's help, bunched them in a sheltered corner on the west side of the butte. A shoulder of the butte offered partial protection from the north, with the butte itself rising sheer above them.

Dagget held a bloody handkerchief to his neck, and seemed awed by the fact that he had been wounded. He glanced up at Shalako. "They might have killed me," he said. "I had just moved."

"A bullet doesn't care who it hits," Shalako said carelessly. "Count yourself lucky."

An Indian suddenly left his shelter and darted forward, and, from his vantage point, von Hallstatt saw him clearly. He tracked him a brief instant, then fired. The Indian stumbled and fell.

A gust of wind whipped across the clearing, scattering the remnants of their fire, driving leaves before it, the dried dead leaves of a bygone year.

Another gust, and then with a roar the storm was upon them, blinding, choking sand that blew down out of the north, obscuring all their surroundings, causing them to gasp for breath.

Shalako grabbed Irina. Quickly he tied a handkerchief over her mouth. He had already pulled his own up to cover his lips, and Fulton had done the same. Von Hallstatt was quick to follow suit, and Count Henri, the last man to scramble up to their hollow among the rocks, had already done so.

Crouching together, they waited. Only Shalako and Fulton held to the rim of the hollow in which they had taken shelter, watching below.

Suddenly, almost drowned in the roar of the wind, Fulton's rifle roared, and Shalako followed.

Von Hallstatt, stumbling against the force of the wind to get into a firing position, felt a sharp tug at his clothing. Roy Harding scrambled to the rim of the cusp, lifted his six-shooter and then as if struck by a gust of wind he was whirled around and fell, tumbling over and over into the bottom of the hollow.

He had been shot through the skull.

Edna Dagget screamed, and threw herself against the rocks, clinging there, far from the fallen man. She screamed and screamed again, but her screams were lost in the wildness of the storm.

The wind mounted to an awful roar, battering at the mountain. Sand bit at their faces like tiny teeth and the wind blew down their throats if they opened their mouths until they were almost strangled by the force of it.

Hunched in their tiny hollow, they waited. And under cover of the storm, the Apaches darted closer and closer.

Twice Shalako fired, and each time he missed, his shooting thrown off by the force of the wind and the dimness of his vision.

The sun was blotted out, and the hollow and all the desert around it were gripped by a curious yellow twilight.

Count Henri struggled to hold the horses, which were plunging and frightened, and Irina went to help him, crooning comfortingly to the horses. Her mares steadied under her hands and held close to her, as if for protection.

Under the howling of the wind, sand rattled against the rock and their clothing, driving with force enough to draw flecks of blood on Edna Dagget's cheeks. Hovering against a wall of the mountain, Shalako tried to shield the action of his Winchester from the sand while he stared with straining eyes into the outer darkness.

Suddenly, during a lull in the wind, he heard the ugly thud of a bullet into flesh and an instant later, the report.

Turning swiftly, Shalako stared up at the mountain, but there was no movement up there but the wind. It was a towering butte, the side broken by weathering, offering ledges and footholds clear to the top. And someone was up there.

Tats-ah-das-ay-go . . . of course.

Someone was crying and Edna was screaming hysterically. Glancing into the hollow, Shalako saw Irina tugging at the body of Count Henri. The Frenchman was down and hurt.

Crossing to her, he bent over the man. It needed only a glance to see that Count Henri was finished. The blood was pumping from a wound in his chest, and all of Irina's efforts could not stop its flow.

He opened his eyes and looked up at them, trying to speak and the roar of the wind drowned out his voice. He collapsed suddenly, and behind him Shalako heard a scream, and a roar of guns.

Wheeling, he saw a dozen Apaches scrambling into the hollow. Fulton had fallen back against the rock wall and was firing both pistols, using fearful execution.

Von Hallstatt, cornered, was clubbing his rifle, and Dagget was rolling on the ground, fighting desperately with an Apache who had leaped upon him. Another had seized Laura and was dragging her toward the edge of the hollow.

Lifting his Winchester, Shalako steadied. An instant he held his aim, then fired.

One of the Indians attacking von Hallstatt dropped

in his tracks. Wheeling, Shalako swung his rifle and shot another man on the rim of the hollow, and then something dropped off the mountain and struck him between the shoulders.

Rolling over, he came up fast and, as the Indian arose, Shalako swung a wicked fist that knocked the Apache sprawling under the plunging hoofs of the horses.

Drawing a Colt, he fired, killing the Indian who had Laura by the hair. At the same instant a gun roared beside him, deafening him with the blast, and he saw another Indian leap back. Irina was on her knees with his rifle in her hands.

Fulton turned suddenly and ducked into the rocks just as a second wave of Indians swarmed into the hollow. Von Hallstatt rushed at them, clubbing his rifle, and when the stock broke, he drew his revolver and fired. He emptied the gun and threw it aside, grabbing up Henri's rifle.

Shalako, berserk with fury, rushed at the Indians, stopped, and opened fire. And then suddenly, they were gone.

They were gone as if they had never been. Except for the dead lying about, the awful howling of the wind, and the three men who remained.

Edna Dagget was dead, struck by a ricocheting bullet. Count Henri was dead. Laura was dazed and shocked, and Bosky Fulton was gone.

"Yellow!" von Hallstatt said. "The man's a coward!"

"No, he's not a coward. He's just a damned selfish brute." Shalako fed shells into his gun, then began gathering the other weapons. "He's looking out for himself, that's all."

There was no escape. The Apaches would still be out

there, waiting for them. And somewhere in the rocks above was *Tats-ah-das-ay-go*, awaiting his opportunity.

The wind roared over and past them, and the sand whipped into their hollow and rattled against the rocks. Irina stood with her horses and the roan, quieting them. Charles Dagget lifted the body of his wife and carried her into a sheltered place behind a boulder where there was some protection from the wind.

Von Hallstatt put down his rifle and crossed to carry Henri to a place beside her.

Shalako picked up the bodies of the three dead Apaches and dropped them down the slope. Only one of them had been armed with a rifle, but that was loaded and put to one side.

Von Hallstatt's coat was ripped from his shoulders, his shirt torn, his face bloody. He had been struck over the head or creased by a bullet that left a nasty scratch on his skull.

Irina left the horses and knelt beside Laura, holding her close. Julia Paige stared at them, dazed and numb with horror at what she had seen.

Shalako walked to the horses and took a canteen from one of them and rinsed his mouth, swallowed a bit, and carried the canteen to von Hallstatt, then to the girls.

Daggett was sitting beside his wife, his head in his hands.

"Get up!" Shalako said roughly. "Get a rifle. They'll be coming back."

Dagget stared up at him. "I don't care," he mumbled. "I don't care at all."

Shalako took him by the shoulder and lifted him to his feet. "I care, I care one hell of a lot, and grief is a luxury you can't afford. There are other women here, man. Now stand ready."

"There should be more dead," von Hallstatt said. "I could have sworn—"

"They carry them off. After dark they'll come for the rest."

"We can't last through another night," Dagget protested. "It is impossible!"

"We'll last," Shalako said. He glanced over at von Hallstatt. "How are you, General?"

"I am well," Hallstatt said, "I am well indeed."

The vast roar of the wind did not cease, nor the wild flurries and gusts that blotted out all about them, obscuring even their own faces from one another. Outside the dust was a veil beyond which they could not see.

Nor did the waiting cease. Eyes red-rimmed and bloodshot, they huddled over their guns at the rim of the hollow with the vast bulk of the butte towering above them, and they waited, squinting into the blasting wind, throats parched, lips dried and cracked until blood came, their skins begrimed and gray.

Peering into the dust and the gathering dark, they waited for the Apaches to come again.

About midnight their water gave out, although they had used little for hours. The night wind roared with awful howls, a mighty wall of wind that threw itself against the mountain and swept brush, leaves and branches before it. Loose rock tumbled from the mountain, and then at last, with dawn, the storm spent itself and the wind died away, and they lay like dead men, staring with glazed and empty eyes upon the scene before them.

———

LIEUTENANT HALL HEARD the firing atop the mountain before the storm broke, but could not place the direction of the sound. Several times earlier he had seemed to hear shots but the sounding board of the mountain was rolling the sound away from him.

When the storm struck, he was in the lee of Gillespie Mountain. On his left was the cliff up which the hunting party had climbed. Not knowing of the dim trail, he did not suspect they might have mounted here.

All tracks in the open were obliterated by the storm, and he supposed all other tracks would be gone. In the desert there are places where tracks may outlive the years, but this he did not know. Unaware of the cliff trail, he could only believe the party had gone on through the pass that led across the range and into Animas Valley.

The storm's arrival demanded they take what shelter they could find, and the bulk of Gillespie proved enough to break the force of the wind and sand. Huddled among the boulders, they made a dry camp.

Hall had been asleep but a short time when he was awakened by Jim Hunt, a half-breed Delaware scout.

"There is fighting on the mountain," Hunt said. "I have heard shooting."

Hall listened, but heard no sound save the roaring of the wind.

"In this storm? Impossible!"

"There was shooting," Hunt insisted.

Hall got up and shook the sand from his boots, then pulled them on. He hesitated, then scratched a brief note on a page of his notebook.

"Could you get to Forsyth?" A couple of frightened prospectors, hurrying out of the area, had told them of the fight near Horseshoe Canyon, and that Forsyth had remained there.

"I go," Hunt said.

When he had gone, Hall did not return to sleep. He got up and walked to the horses. They were restless, and kept tugging toward the north.

Brannigan, who was standing horse guard, came up to him. "I think there's water over there, sir," he said. "Want me to have a look?"

"Yes, but be careful."

The lieutenant stood guard while Brannigan made his search, and he was thinking of Laura Davis. He had danced with her once when she had been touring Army posts with her father. It seemed impossible that she could be here, in such a place.

It was nearly light and the wind was dying when Brannigan returned.

"There's water, Lieutenant. About a half a mile from here, right over at the foot of the mountain." He scratched his jaw, which itched from the stubble of whiskers and the dust. "Good water, too."

When the troop had watered their horses and filled their canteens, they made coffee while Hall swept the cliffs with his field glass.

"Something up there," he said finally. "Looks like a body hanging among the rocks well up toward the top."

He stared through the glass, genuinely puzzled, for there was a spot of brightness there, brighter than any reflection from a rifle barrel.

Brannigan walked over to him, holding a cup of coffee. "Lieutenant . . . this is for you." He squinted at the cliff. "Want I should go up there? I'm a right curious man, Lieutenant."

"Let somebody else go. You've done your bit for the day."

"If the lieutenant pleases, I'd take it as a favor. I've a thought we'll find there's been a fight up there."

"All right, Brannigan. If you wish."

———

WHEN FORSYTH FOLLOWED Jim Hunt back to the foot of Gillespie Mountain, the troop awaited him beside the body of Bosky Fulton.

The body was horribly mutilated.

"One of the men said it was Bosky Fulton, a gunman," Hall commented. "His pockets were stuffed with money and jewels, sir. Must be fifty thousand dollars' worth or more."

Forsyth looked down at the body. He had known Fulton by sight, and had a sharp dislike for the man, but he could feel nothing but pity now. Fulton had died very slowly, and he had died hard.

"He was jammed among the rocks, sir. Brannigan says he must have been winged, and when he fell, he fell with his gun arm under him, caught between the rocks so he couldn't get himself out.

"His right arm was pinned, and the bullet had gone through his left arm so that he couldn't use it. The Indian must have followed him down and slowly cut him into slices like that."

Literally, the body was covered with blood, blood that had flowed from a thousand small cuts, cuts made deliberately and with care.

"I would wish that on no man, although judging by his pockets, the man was a thief as well as a murderer."

"There's others up there, Colonel. Brannigan heard

voices, but after what he'd seen he wasn't sure he wanted to investigate. He couldn't make out what they were talking, but it sounded like English."

"There's a trail up there," McDonald suggested. "We passed it back down the canyon."

"All right," Forsyth said, "we'll take a look. Mount your men, Lieutenant."

———

SHALAKO SHOOK VON Hallstatt's shoulder. "Better wake up, General," he said. "I think we're alone. I think the Indians have pulled out."

Sunrise was two hours gone, and the sky was blue and clear, only a few scattered puffballs of cloud hung against the still blue. The air after the storm was startlingly clear.

No smoke could be seen, nor anything else. Down where the camp had been before the final retreat, birds were scattered about the clearing, picking at crumbs left from their previous meals.

"We've got to have water," Shalako added.

He took the reins of Irina's horses and told Dagget to lead the roan. Then he led the way out of the hollow and down onto the flat where the camp had been.

A few spots of blood were visible, but there were no bodies at all now. The three Apaches they had thrown out of the hollow had been carried away during the night. Carrying his Winchester ready in his hands, and wary of every movement, Shalako led the way.

There was no trouble. All was still. The last of the dust had settled, and the warm sun brought out the smell of pine and cedar. When they reached the spring they dismounted and filled their canteens.

"There's no coffee left, not even the old grounds, but there's tea." Irina looked up at him. "Shall I make tea?"

"Sure . . . at a time like this tea beats anything. Strong black tea, hot as you can drink it. The best thing for shock of any kind, and the best stimulant there is for what we've been through."

He glanced around at the small group. The others were as unlike themselves as von Hallstatt. Julia Paige looked haggard and drawn, ten years older than she probably was. Laura Davis was tired, and only Irina seemed fresh, although her eyes were unnaturally large, and the hollows were deep around them.

"Are they gone?" von Hallstatt asked.

Shalako stood up, his eyes ranging the brush and rocks. "I think so. The Army's coming . . . they would know that before we would, and they would move out. Anyway, they probably decided what we had to take wasn't worth the price."

Except for *Tats-ah-das-ay-go*. He had paid no price at all. He was detached, a thing apart. He was like the wind or the rain, he came and he went and one did not make rules for him.

He might remain behind. It would be like him.

"We'll take no chances," Shalako said. "The one who killed Harris might still be here."

The heat seemed to have blown away with the wind, and the slight warmth from the early sun was only enough to dispel the chill. The birds continued to chirp and call in the brush and trees, and Shalako moved out to one side and sat down, his rifle across his knees.

Von Hallstatt came over and crouched beside him, stoking his pipe.

From where they sat they could look westward over a

wild and broken land, the raw-backed mountains, devoid of vegetation for the most part, or scattered with the grays and faint greens of desert growth. The nearer pines and cedars covered only a limited area, and some of those had died and fallen into ruin over the broken red rocks.

"Without you," von Hallstatt said, "we should have been killed . . . all of us."

"The land is hard. A man cannot fight this country, he lives *with* it, or he dies. A man learns to become a part of it, to live like the desert plants do, almost without water, and to use every bit of available cover, like the desert animals do. And to fight an Indian, as Washington tried to tell Braddock, a man has to become like an Indian."

"You spoke once of Saxe, of Vegetius. They are writers on tactics, the knowledge of command. Were you a soldier?"

"I read them." He built a cigarette with careful fingers, his eyes restless in searching the rocks. "When I was sixteen I pulled out from home and fought the last two years of the Civil War with the Union forces, a cavalry outfit. I came out a lieutenant. Didn't figure I knew enough, so I started reading tactics. When the war was over I went to Africa and fought with the Boers in the Basuto War . . . maybe six months. After that I served as a colonel under Shir Ali in Afghanistan in the fighting after the death of Dost Mohammed."

"Henri thought he knew you."

"He saw me twice, I think. Once during the Franco-Prussian War when MacMahon sent me to Metz. I was to take a message through to Bazaine."

"But that was impossible! Metz was surrounded."

Shalako glanced at him. "I went back and forth three times . . . no trouble. Your German sentries should serve on the Indian frontier for a while, General. Any Apache or Kiowa could steal the buttons off their coats."

"And then?"

"The French lost. I shucked my uniform, produced my American papers and went to Paris. Stayed awhile, and went to London. . . ."

Julia Paige suddenly rushed up to them. "Are you mad? Are you going to sit there all day drinking tea and smoking? Or are we going to get out of here?" Her voice rose stridently.

"There is time, Julia," von Hallstatt replied. "We are as safe here as we would be moving, and the Army will come. And then, we must arrange burial for our friends."

She started to protest, then turned away, dragging her feet. "We will be killed," she said dully. "We will all be killed."

Shalako tried to hold his eyes open. He was desperately, brutally tired. There had been too little sleep for him in too long a time. The short rest behind the ruined cabin, the other sleep he had after leaving the hunting party at the ranch amounted to very little, and in between there had been riding, fighting, dust, sun, and struggle. And before that, a long stretch of living on ragged nerve in the mountains of Mexico.

Yet he was uneasy. He scanned the shattered shoulders of Elephant Butte and the edges of the canyon with careful attention. The Apaches had gone . . . his every sense told him that, told him also that the Army was coming. The trouble was that *Tats-ah-das-ay-go* had been out there, and no rule applied to him. The others might go, but he would stay . . . or he might seem to leave and then return.

He lived with the others, but always alone and near them. He sat in their councils, but rarely spoke, and when he fought, it was always alone. Even the Apaches feared him, feared his skill as a fighting man and his uncertain temper.

"Pile on some brush," he said to Dagget. "If we raise a big smoke the Army will find us sooner."

"Couldn't one of us ride to meet them?" Laura suggested. "They might pass us by."

"We'll chance it. We must stay together. There is danger yet."

Irina brought them each a cup of tea. She sat down beside Shalako. "Did I hear you telling Frederick you had been in Paris? What did you do there?"

"Whatever one does in Paris. When I came there it was a few months before the war broke out, and I had a little money. I used to go to a small café in the Avenue Clichy called the Guerbois."

He glanced at her. "I hadn't much education, you know. There were no schools where I grew up, at least none to speak of. But I'd learned to read, and could write a little, and I started reading stories."

"In *French*?"

"Yes. I read French better than English, and German almost as well. Spoke both of them a sight better than I could read, though."

"But . . . I do not understand. You said there were no schools?"

"No schools to speak of. Only I was raised in Texas, not in California, like some folks say. I was born in California, but went with my folks to Texas. Have you ever been to San Antonio? Well, outside of San Antonio there's a place called Castroville, and a town called D'Hanis, too.

"Castroville and D'Hanis . . . they were founded by a group of colonists brought over from Alsace, only some of them were Swiss, German, Dutch, and just about everything, by a man named Count Henri de Castro in 1844.

"Old buildings stand there yet, and some of the houses are just like in the old country. Folks around there mostly spoke French and German, and about the time I was learning to talk, we moved into that area.

"D'Hanis was the last town . . . nothing between there and the Rio Grande except wild country, wild cattle, and wilder Indians. Well, I started talking down there, and I could speak French and German before I could speak proper English. Comes of playing with youngsters talking those languages.

"Sometimes I sat alongside when their folks taught them from books. Like I said, there was no proper school, but I learned to read some French before I did English."

"You were telling me about Paris."

"Yes. I went to that café on the Avenue Clichy, and I met some fellows there . . . they were painters. One of them they thought so much of they used to save him a couple of tables. His name was Manet."

"Oh, yes! I have heard of him. A friend of mine bought a painting of his in Paris. This friend was an old friend of the family of Degas. Did you know him?"

"The aristocrat? I knew him. And that other fellow who came there sometimes. I read some of his books . . . Zola, his name was, Émile Zola."

She glanced at von Hallstatt, who had gone to the fire.

"Do not mention that name to Frederick. He detests him. Calls him a Socialist and a wild man . . . but I like his books."

"He told me some books to read, gave me a few in fact, just after a party we had to celebrate my joining up. It was only a few weeks that I knew them. They were a wild lot, always arguing. I am no painter or writer and understood none of it."

Lethargy settled heavily upon him. Several times he nodded, blinking his eyes open quickly, afraid that she might see . . . and she had.

"Why don't you sleep, Shalako? Frederick can keep watch . . . and I want to brush my hair."

She left him and returned to the fire. Shalako hitched himself into a more comfortable position and slowly searched the rocks again. He could not remember ever being so tired . . . there was a low murmur of voices from the group at the fire.

The Army would be coming soon.

Irina went to the saddlebags that held all that remained of her personal belongings, and found her comb and brush. These, at least, she had salvaged. Von Hallstatt was helping Dagget build up the fire. Laura was brushing her clothing, trying to make herself presentable. Von Hallstatt paused from time to time to look at the rocks, and Julia merely sat and waited, her cup of tea untouched.

TATS-AH-DAS-AY-GO LAY UPON a bare rocky slope within less than seventy yards of the fire. His entire body was in plain sight, its length broken only by an outcropping of sandstone that partly obscured his legs, and a small bit of prickly pear near his shoulder.

He had been lying there for nearly an hour, absolutely immovable. Several times during that period both von Hallstatt and Shalako had looked directly at him without seeing him.

The bare slope was innocent of cover. It was not a place one examined, and the Apache knew that. Several times he could have fired . . . he could have killed one, perhaps more. But he waited.

Now, at last . . . he moved.

He made no sound, but when he stopped moving he was farther to the left and nearer the canyon. His eyes had found their target, for one of the girls was picking up a towel . . . he had watched women and girls brush their hair and wash their faces around the forts too many times not to know what she planned.

The fire was but a short distance from the spring, which was concealed around a cluster of rock. He watched her walk around the rocks and disappear, and for several minutes he remained where he was, watching the others.

And most of all he watched the man who sat asleep against the rocks.

Was he actually asleep? Or was he only seeming to be asleep? This was the man who brought the rain . . . all the Indians had heard the story. He was also the man who had known the name of *Tats-ah-das-ay-go,* which was a kind of magic.

Finally, he moved from his position, went back into the rocks and circled around to watch the girl at the spring. She was bathing her hands and face, then she began combing out her hair. It was very long hair, and very beautiful. The Apache moved closer, making no sound.

He would kill her now, and when someone came to find her, he would kill another with his bow.

Yet *Tats-ah-das-ay-go* was uneasy. He wished he could see the man sleeping near the rocks. He waited an instant and moved nearer.

He had killed the big man with the beard. He had killed the man on guard on the cliff edge, and he had killed the man with the guns, the one who had fallen into the rocks.

Following the man down he had found him trapped there, and he had spent hours with him, gagging him with a handful of rough grass torn from a tiny ledge among the rocks. The man had died very hard, and very long. In the end all his courage was gone and he was whimpering as a child would whimper.

Now he would kill the girl, and then one other. After that he would go, for the pony soldiers were coming. He had been watching from the rocks when they sent a man up to get the one he had just killed.

It had been a temptation to kill the man climbing the rocks right before the eyes of the soldiers. Only they had rifles which shot very far, and the red-faced man was there, the one who rode with McDonald. That man was a very good shot, and the risk was too great. It was not worth it.

He crept nearer. The girl was close now, and she was brushing her hair over and over again and was engrossed in that. She looked like a girl who thought of a man.

———

Shalako opened his eyes suddenly and from long training he did not move until his eyes had searched the terrain about him, and then he turned his head to look toward the fire.

Von Hallstatt was drinking tea. Dagget was searching

for brush and sticks to add to the signal fire. Julia sat very still, hunched over and face down on her arms, while Laura was still painstakingly brushing her clothes. He could have been asleep only a few minutes.

Irina was nowhere in sight.

He got to his feet and walked to the fire, and he was frightened. He looked carefully around before he spoke, not wishing to alarm them needlessly. "Where's Irina?" he asked, after a minute.

"Combing her hair," Laura said, "at the spring."

He glanced toward the pile of rocks that concealed the spring from their eyes. Would these people never learn that for one to be out of sight of the others was dangerous, that danger was ever-present? Yet he had himself relaxed, so the fault was his as well. He started around the rock, then halted and circled in the other direction. No one at the fire seemed to be paying any attention to him, or to notice anything odd about his actions.

He climbed among the rocks, then lay still, straining his ears to hear.

Water falling . . . the click of something placed upon a rock . . . perhaps a hair brush. Ahead of him lay several large loose stones on top of the rock over which he was crawling. Using them as partial cover, he lifted his head slowly.

At first he saw only the spring, a trickle of water from among the rocks into a basin, after which it ran off down a shallow watercourse toward Park Canyon, some distance off.

Irina was seated on a flat rock near the spring, and she was brushing her hair. Her reflection could be seen in the small pool where the water fell . . . a more peaceful scene could not be imagined.

He started to speak, but something held him back. And then he saw the Indian.

He was taller than most Apaches, yet broad in the shoulders and amazingly thick through the chest. His arms and legs were powerfully muscled, and he moved now like a cat, his eyes riveted on the unsuspecting girl.

He was directly opposite the girl, and there was no way to get a good shot at him.

Tats-ah-das-ay-go was intent only upon the girl by the spring. Knife in hand he moved down over the rocks and poised for an instant, and in that instant, two things happened.

Warned by some instinct, Irina turned suddenly, and a flicker of movement from Shalako caught the Indian's eye.

Tats-ah-das-ay-go's eyes switched to Shalako, and in that moment the latter dove from the top of his rock. The Indian tried to turn, but his feet were among the rocks and, in turning, he lost balance.

Shalako landed before him even as Irina sprang back. She did not scream. Her eyes went quickly around and she saw men, circling warily.

"Tats-ah-das-ay-go!" Shalako said softly. He held his knife low, cutting edge up. "I shall kill you now!"

The Apache moved in suddenly, his blade darting with a stabbing thrust like the strike of a rattler, and the point ripped a gash in the buckskin of Shalako's breeches at the hip. A little low, a little wide.

They closed suddenly, and rolled over on the sand, stabbing and thrusting; then they came up, facing each other. There was a fleck of blood on Shalako's shirt-front. He sprang suddenly, and the Indian leaped back to escape his thrust, and they fell into the brush and cacti, then were out on the rocks.

Irina, her face white and strained, could not cry out, she could not scream, she could only stare as if hypnotized by the men before her.

Circling, thrusting . . . another fleck of blood showed on Shalako, on his arm. The Apache was incredibly swift, incredibly agile. His flat, hard face, with its thick cheekbones and flat black eyes, was like a mask, showing no emotion.

Shalako moved, seemed to slip, and the Indian sprang in. Instantly Shalako turned and swung with his left fist, catching the Indian on the side of the neck and knocking him sprawling.

Yet the Apache came up swiftly, lunged low for the soft parts of the body, and Shalako slapped the blade aside and lunged. His blade went into the Indian's side, but *Tats-ah-das-ay-go* swung around, striking swiftly with his blade.

The blade went into Shalako, but Shalako struck again with his fist and they both fell. Shalako lost his grip on the knife when his fist slammed against a rock with brutal force. The Indian sprang at him and Shalako rolled over and came to his feet, empty-handed. The Indian lunged to get close and Shalako sidestepped, caught the Indian's wrist, and threw him into a heap of brush.

From beyond the rocks there was a sudden shout of alarm, and Dagget cried out, "Irina! What's the matter? What's happening!"

There was a flurry of feet, and, for an instant, the

Apache hesitated, then wheeled and ran into the rocks, and vanished.

Shalako went after him.

From somewhere down the valley came the sound of a bugle. Dagget, von Hallstatt, and the women came around the boulder.

In that instant, the Quick-Killer came suddenly into view, racing over the rocks like a goat, heading for Elephant Butte Canyon. And then he stopped, for suddenly Shalako appeared, almost in front of him.

The Indian wheeled and raced up the side of the butte itself, with Shalako behind him. The Indian turned, toppled a rock toward Shalako, then went on up.

Down below, von Hallstatt stood, rifle in hand, so engrossed in the scene before him that he forgot the rifle and did not think to fire.

The two men vanished, appeared again, and suddenly they were facing each other atop the butte.

The sun was hot, and there was no wind. Atop the butte the rock was flat, here and there the thin sheet of surface rock had broken down and the fragments had been blown away by wind. There were no plants here, no growth of any kind except one gnarled dwarf cedar that clung to the far lip, a few feet below the edge.

Behind Shalako, who had circled somewhat in climbing, the cliff fell steeply away for more than a thousand feet. His shirt, torn before, ripped more in scrambling up the rocks, was now in shreds. Shalako ripped the rags from his back so as not to impede his arms in their movements.

The Indian stood, legs apart, one foot forward, staring at him.

Around them was the vast bowl of the sun-hot sky, below them the awful jumble of broken, jagged rock and desert, mountain, and canyon. They were alone, under the sky, a buzzard the only spectator.

Each understood what was to happen now, each knew that a man would die . . . perhaps two men. Each knew it would be settled here.

The Indian was supremely confident. He had fought many times with members of his tribe or other Apache tribes, and with Mexicans and Yaquis. Yet he was wary of the American, for the man had thrown him into the rocks. He had proved a puzzling, dangerous fighter.

Tats-ah-das-ay-go gripped his knife tighter and moved toward Shalako.

Remote sounds could be heard from below. But on the butte it was very still. Shalako's mouth was dry and he gripped and ungripped his fists, watching every move of the Apache.

The man had a knife, which he was skilled at using. Shalako circled to the right, causing the Indian to turn to keep in front of him. He feinted a move, but the Indian merely watched him and was not fooled.

The heat was frightful. Sweat began to trickle down Shalako's chest. His lips tasted salt from the sweat of his face.

Shalako moved his left foot forward, gaining a few inches, crouching a little. The Apache feinted, then came in fast. Unable to knock the knife blow aside, Shalako struck it down, catching the Apache's elbow in the grip of his hand.

Closing his powerful grip on the man's elbow, he dug his fingers, seeking the funny bone, to find it and paralyze the Indian's arm. For a moment then they fought, straining every muscle, and then Shalako, retaining his grip on the arm, suddenly yielded and stepped back, throwing the Apache off balance.

Shalako hooked a short, vicious blow to the face as the Indian fell into him, and then another. The Indian fought to bring the knife up, but then Shalako's seeking fingers found the nerve he wanted and began to grind upon it.

The Apache cried out and tried to break free, but Shalako crowded upon him, forcing the Indian to move back to keep from falling, and no matter how desperately the Indian struggled, he stayed with him.

Suddenly the Indian cried out and, opening his hand, let go of the knife.

It fell, rattling upon the rocks. Wheeling, the Apache sprang for it, but Shalako was first and kicked the knife, sending it spinning off into space. It caught the sunlight, winked brightly, then fell down among the rocks far below.

Shalako slugged the Indian as they closed and he felt the clawlike hands creeping toward his eyes. Wildly, bitterly, desperately they fought, their bodies greasy with sweat and blood, their faces straining only inches apart.

Again Shalako yielded suddenly, falling back and throwing the Indian over him to the rock. Swiftly, he came up as the Indian sprang on him. The powerful hands grasped his throat, his head was pushed back, he felt the brutal thumbs sinking into the flesh of his throat, and then he jerked his two arms up inside the Indian's arms smashing them apart and away from his throat. The Indian fell forward, and Shalako rolled over and came to his knees as the Indian leaped at him, swinging a vicious kick at Shalako's head.

Throwing himself against the Indian's anchor leg, he threw the Quick-Killer violently to the rock, and Shalako staggered to his feet.

Under the blazing sun, he waited for the Indian to get up. His lungs heaved at the thin air, gasping for breath. The advantage was momentarily his, but he lacked the breath to go forward, and the Apache got to his feet.

For an instant, they stood staring at each other across the rock of the small butte. Lungs heaving, they began to circle. The Quick-Killer sprang, and Shalako grabbed his wrist, swinging the arm back and under, then forcing it up the Apache's back in a hammerlock.

Shalako pushed the Apache's wrist higher across his back, then began with all his strength to force the Indian's right wrist over to his right shoulder. Once the Indian grunted, his face went bloodless and he tried to turn to relieve the pressure, but Shalako blocked the turning and, bending suddenly at the knees, he heaved upward with all his strength and both felt and heard the bone crack.

The Indian cried out, his face white with pain, and he swung free, staggered, and tried to grasp Shalako with his left hand. Shalako swung and hit him, and the Indian lost his footing and fell back. He hit the edge of the cliff above the desert in a sitting position, his broken arm still grotesquely behind him, and then he toppled back, his black eyes still upon those of Shalako, and then he fell slowly over backward into space.

The last thing Shalako saw was the eyes of the Indian,

the eyes of *Tats-ah-das-ay-go*, the Quick-Killer, fastened upon his.

As the Apache fell, Shalako cried out suddenly, almost in anguish, in admiration: "Warrior! Brother!"

And he spoke in Apache.

Shalako heard *Tats-ah-das-ay-go*'s wild cry as he struck, somewhere far below, before the body bounded out again, to fall sheer for hundreds of feet.

And then he was alone upon the mountaintop, and there was only the heat, the sweat, and his lungs gasping, crying for air.

Shalako stood alone there, looking off across the hills, then he lifted his eyes toward the sun-blazing sky, almost as if in prayer.

They were waiting below, he could see them standing there, staring up at him, shading their eyes against the sun's glare.

He could see Irina, von Hallstatt, Dagget, Laura, and Julia. The Army was there, too, the sun glinting on the glossy shoulders of their horses, reflecting from their rifles. They stood there in a long, winding column, several hundred of them, and he was glad to see them.

He climbed down slowly, the sweat streaming into his eyes and causing them to smart from the salt, and when he reached the bottom he walked to where his guns were and picked them up.

They stood watching him, none of them coming up to him, and he walked toward them.

He looked up at Colonel Forsyth. "Howdy," he said. "I guess we can go now."

The colonel started to speak . . . desperately he wanted to know what had happened up there atop the butte, but that this man lived was evidence enough.

"All right, then. We shall go."

Von Hallstatt started to speak, but Shalako walked past him and held Tally's stirrup for Irina. She hesitated an instant, then allowed him to help her into the saddle. Her eyes searched his face and, as the rest of them mounted, he swung his leg over Mohammet and pulled up beside her.

"This is my country," he said. "This and California."

She did not speak, but listened, looking down at her nails. They were broken, no longer perfectly manicured, but they were a woman's hands, strong hands, capable hands. They were hands of beauty, but hands of more than beauty, they were hands with which to do.

"It will be different for you."

"I know."

They rode on, and when they reached the road that turned eastward toward Fort Cummings, they drew up.

Colonel Forsyth rode back to them, von Hallstatt beside him. The colonel's eyes went from Shalako's to Irina's.

"You are stopping?" Forsyth asked.

"Our way lies westward."

Forsyth started to speak, then was silent. Von Hallstatt hesitated, his face stiff and cold. Then he said, "It is a good way, my friend, a good way." He held out his hand, and Shalako took it.

"Irina"—his eyes held upon hers for a moment— "Irina . . . good-bye."

"Good-bye, Frederick."

Von Hallstatt turned his eyes again upon Shalako. Then the Prussian saluted, snapping the salute in the approved military fashion, and Shalako returned it.

As they rode off, Forsyth said, "I did not know he was a soldier."

"He was," von Hallstatt said dryly. "And he is!"

When they had gone a few miles Irina said, "I do not look like a bride."

Shalako shifted his grip on the lead ropes of Damper and the roan. "You will," he said. "You will!"

WHAT IS LOUIS L'AMOUR'S LOST TREASURES?

Louis L'Amour's Lost Treasures is a project created to release some of the author's more unconventional manuscripts from the family archives.

Currently included in the project are *Louis L'Amour's Lost Treasures: Volume 1,* published in 2017, and *Volume 2,* which will be published in the fall of 2019. These books contain both finished and unfinished short stories, unfinished novels, literary and motion picture treatments, notes, and outlines. They are a wide selection of the many works Louis was never able to publish during his lifetime.

In 2018 we released *No Traveller Returns,* L'Amour's never-before-seen first novel, which was written between 1938 and 1942. In the future, there may be a selection of even more L'Amour titles.

Additionally, many notes and alternate drafts to Louis's well-known and previously published novels and short stories will now be included as "bonus feature" postscripts within the books that they relate to. For example, the Lost Treasures postscript to *Last of the Breed* will contain early notes on the story, the short story that was discovered to be a missing piece of the novel, the history of the novel's inspiration and creation, and information about unproduced motion picture and comic book versions.

An even more complete description of the Lost Treasures project, along with a number of examples of what is in the books, can be found at louislamourslosttreasures .com. The website also contains a good deal of exclusive material, such as even more pieces of unknown stories that were too short or too incomplete to include in the Lost Treasures books, plus personal photos, scans of original documents, and notes.

All of the works that contain Lost Treasures project materials will display the Louis L'Amour's Lost Treasures banner and logo.

LOUIS L'AMOUR'S LOST TREASURES

POSTSCRIPT

By Beau L'Amour

The Lost Treasures Postscript material available for *Shalako* falls into three categories: Louis's inspiration for certain aspects of the story, a controversy over its premise that cropped up more than once, and the dramatic story of getting the movie made; it was groundbreaking, one of the earliest "independent" features of the modern era.

My father traced his initial interest in the subject matter of *Shalako* to a number of experiences he had during his years as an itinerant laborer and hobo in the 1920s. The first, and probably the most influential, was the time he spent as a teenager in West Texas skinning dead cattle with a man he referred to as a "wolf hunter." The man lived in a house not far from Lubbock's South Plains Fairgrounds, where Louis, his parents, and his adopted brother were camped while desperately searching for work. In a 1979 letter, Louis explained:

> There had been a terrible drouth [drought] and many cattle died and I hired out to an old wolf hunter to help. It was a very unpleasant

job, but jobs were hard to get and I needed the money. But it turned out to be one of the best things I ever did. The old man for whom I worked was a white man who had been raised by the Apaches. He had ridden on war parties with Geronimo and Nana when he was sixteen and seventeen. He was nearly seventy-nine when I knew him. Nobody came near us because of what we were doing (some of the cattle had been dead for a while!) and every night by the campfire he talked about his time with the Apaches: how they lived, tracked, fought, etc. Much of what there was about Apaches in HONDO and SHALAKO came from his stories. He had been there.

Louis hitchhiked through the New Mexico "boot heel" not long afterward, and then again a year or so later while traveling west from Texas after his first trip to sea. He was kicked off a freight train in Steins Pass, New Mexico, and ended up both walking and hitchhiking to Phoenix to meet up with his parents.

Though it was hard traveling of a sort he wouldn't have chosen if he'd had the option, it was a good way to see the country. It's worth remembering that at the time my father made these journeys—hopping freights, walking and catching occasional rides in automobiles—the landscape was still much as it had been in the time period of the novel *Shalako*. It had not been fifty years, the roads were dirt or gravel, and any suggestion of civilization was thinly spread.

Louis returned once more to the boot heel country in 1959. On that trip he and my mother stopped off in Tucson to visit the set of *Heller in Pink Tights,* the film being made from his novel *Heller with a Gun.* After a few days with director George Cukor and stars Anthony Quinn, Sophia Loren, and Steve Forrest, they continued on, back to Steins Pass and points south.

On the same trip they visited Silver City, where they met with Tom Threepersons, often considered the last of the Old West lawmen. They then drove on to Lincoln, Fort Sumner, and Santa Rosa—all places where Dad had lived and worked in the months following the cattle-skinning job. Heading into the northern part of the state, they visited Mora (which shows up in *The Daybreakers*), Cimarron, Taos, and Santa Fe. On the way home they passed through Springerville and Show Low, Arizona. Photographs from that trip also place them at one of New Mexico's Salinas Missions and at Hannagan Meadow on the Mogollon Rim in Arizona.

This sort of rambling car trip was typical of my parents in those days, and everywhere they went Dad would talk to old-timers, check out the local history in small libraries and historical societies, and generally acquaint himself with the countryside.

By late 1960 Louis was hard at work on *Shalako,* utilizing the research he had accumulated both before and during these travels. In December he, uncharacteristically, decided that the story didn't have enough "characterization" and decided to rewrite it immediately.

Throughout Louis's career there are a small number of references to significant revisions on a finished work such as this, but very few of the original manuscript pages remain in existence. I suspect that he threw old drafts away in order to avoid any confusion. He was not very good at filing or labeling things, and the possibility that pieces of two different drafts might get shuffled together was a chance he wouldn't have wanted to take.

The process of revision took about four weeks. Dad did not touch-type and had no secretary, so that meant he had to retype the entire manuscript from beginning to end. He wrapped the novel up by mid-January of 1961 and, as was typical, he did not initially like it very much.

A note from his journal on February 2nd relates: "Roberts [a Bantam employee] says: 'I think it is one of the best you have ever done. It has vigor and clarity and I'm sure you enjoyed writing it.'" Louis's comment, typed immediately below, reads: "I do not think it is one of my best, by far."

In the late 1950s and early 1960s, Louis attempted to expand his work beyond writing Westerns. By 1962 he was painfully learning that this particular goal was not going to be easily attained. Both because of his growing success and because of publishers' reluctance to experiment with anything new, the message was fairly uniform: Stick to the Westerns.

With a family to support, out-and-out rebellion was not an option for Louis, nor did he wish to leave traditional Westerns completely behind. So a decade or more passed before he began pushing his audience's acceptance with outside-the-envelope books like *The Californios* and *Sackett's Land*. Regardless, there were a few careful experiments with stories like 1966's *The Broken Gun* (a contemporary Western/mystery), 1964's *Kiowa Trail* (a traditional Western with a subplot in a British boarding school), and *Shalako*.

Dad had no lofty motives; he just wanted to write a wider variety of material, or at the very least to not always be stuck in the cow camps and boomtowns that were typical Western fare. Although a number of other Western writers were also pushing the boundaries in this same time period, *Shalako*, in its mash-up of European safari and Apache outbreak, quickly demonstrated that even slight deviations in the genre could become controversial.

In the summer of 1963, the reaction of some members of the Western Writers of America to the novel's departure from the norms of the Western genre sparked the following comment in Louis's journal:

> Write [wrote] a reply to a
> judgment by the judges in the WWA
> contest where they spoke of my
> "improbable" Western characters,
> but said nice things about the
> book.

Here is his reply in its entirety:

> An Open Letter to the Old
> Buckaroos,
> Gentlemen:
> First allow me to congratulate you
> on the selection of Fred Grove's
> COMMANCHE CAPTIVES, and Hal G.
> Evarts' MASSACRE CREEK. I have read
> both novels and enjoyed them very

much, and believe both are among
the best tradition of the frontier
novel.

However, I must take exception
to a phrase in your comments on my
novel, SHALAKO. You say: "Despite a
highly improbable cast . . ." and
then you list the German Baron, the
French count, the senator's
daughter, etc. who made up the
cast, the hunting party which
figured largely in my novel. For
some reason you call these people
highly improbable. Unfortunately, I
can only put this down to a
complete forgetfulness of what was
happening in the American West.

After living in the West much of
my life, and years of research in
the field, I can think of no
Western cast I would consider
improbable. One of the great charms
of the West, and one of the things
that cause me to continue to write
about it, as well as one of the
reasons people like to read about
it, was that the West was a place
where the improbable happened every
day.

However, as to my cast: let me
remind the judges that in the
summer of 1855, some thirty years
before my story, Sir George Gore,

of Sligo, Ireland, came hunting buffalo. He had 43 men in his party, 112 horses, 12 yokes of oxen, 14 dogs, 6 wagons, and 21 carts, many of the carts loaded with the finest luxury goods money could buy.

Sir George went hunting in the heart of Sioux country, and if he did not have the trouble my party of hunters had it was perhaps due to a guide named Jim Bridger.

Arriving a few years before, but living on the edge of the Dakota Badlands at the same time as my story, was the Frenchman who founded the town of Medora, named for his wife. This was Antoine-Marie-Vincent-Manca de Valombrosa, otherwise known as the Marquis de Mores.

The handsome marquis, an improbable character indeed, built a chateau where he entertained forty or fifty of Europe's greatest nobility. They hunted buffalo, antelope, and grizzlies. Many of them were accompanied by their wives, and the wife of the marquis, the Baroness Medora von Hoffman, was the daughter of a New York banker.

Quite incidentally, the baroness

came west with the fervent ambition to kill a grizzly with a pistol. A noted horse woman and an excellent shot, she lived for many years after, so I do not believe she tried it. Not to say that it couldn't be done.

Living in the same area at the same time, was another extremely improbable character named Teddy Roosevelt.

However, the marquis to make certain of his improbability, engaged in a minor range war, including a gun battle in which he and a companion killed one man and wounded another. So here we have an improbable French nobleman engaging in an improbable gun battle, and in a very improbable way, winning the fight.

Ten years earlier than my story, the Grand Duke Alexis came hunting. Gen. Sheridan supervised the party for him, with Buffalo Bill as guide. Accompanying the party were Consul Bodisco, Chancellor Machen, Admiral Possiet, Gen. George A. Custer, Lt. Stordegraff, Count Olsonfieff, and . . . others, including that same Col. George A. Forsyth who figured in my story.

Among others, touring or hunting

before and after the period of my
novel, were the Viscountess of
Avonmore, the Earl of Dunraven, Lady
Guest, Lady Duffas Hardy, Lady Rose
Pender (she rode from Cheyenne to
Rapid City and then to Miles City in
a buggy in 1883, the year following
my story), the Baron of Swansea, and
the party of the Duke of Sutherland.
There were others too numerous to
mention. In my files I have a list
of forty-nine such groups and there
were many more.

Visiting the Marquis de Mores at
about this time was the very
improbable character named Galiot
Francois Edmond, Baron de Mandat-
Grancey, who not only toured the
West but wrote an excellent book
about it called COWBOYS AND
COLONELS.

Another equally improbable
visitor was Oscar Wilde, who stood
at the bar in velvet knee breeches
belting the juice with the miners
of Leadville and nearby points.
Later, he even shared a bottled
lunch with a group of miners at the
bottom of a mine shaft.

The Apache raid and the
resulting army maneuvers as related
in my story are factual. The names
of the officers, the Indians and

all the places are factual. Even
the Apache called the Quick-Killer
was a real warrior, and known to be
as I have written of him. The
locale of the story is correct down
to the finest point, and I invite
any reader to look over the ground
in that southwestern corner of New
Mexico below Lordsberg.

What the judges objected to in
my story was not the writing, which
could be much, much better, but the
history. True, I used a fictional
device in placing one of the many
such parties of hunters in the
midst of an actual Indian outbreak,
but this is accepted practice.

The judges added this unkindest
cut of all: "L'Amour all but
convinced us that it could have
happened."

Gentlemen, I stand by my story.
You go back and read it again. I
did convince you.

In addition to the finished letter, Dad's notes contain
some twenty other instances of prominent European
men and women traveling throughout the Wild West.
Restraint seems to have taken over at some point in the
rebuttal process.

Louis often chafed against the edges of what the genre
would let him do. For a long time the frontier depicted in
Western fiction seemed to exist in an isolated fantasy-

land somehow separate not only from the rest of the world but from the civilization lying just hundreds of miles away in the Eastern states. Foreigners in Western fiction (exactly who was "foreign" in a young nation of immigrants is a mind bogglingly open question) were only allowed to play certain clichéd roles. The acceptable era was often limited to a brief thirty-year period from the end of the Civil War to the "closing of the frontier." And many Western writers tended to obsess over the cattle business and military matters.

Those examples are just an indication of the mindset that defined the narrowest definition of the genre. Thankfully, there is also a great deal of work that exists outside those parameters. However, the controversy over whether it was acceptable in fiction for Europeans to do in the West as they were well known to do in Africa followed *Shalako* from the medium of prose into film.

Near the end of 1962 Universal Studios bought an option on *Shalako*. An option is a contract with producers or studios to lease the film rights to a story while they discover if they can pull together a script and a cast. Initially, there was some suggestion that Jimmy Stewart was under consideration for the title role. It was a traditional Hollywood studio deal and a traditional Hollywood studio star, a formula that ten years earlier would have worked like a charm. In this case, though, the option eventually lapsed with nothing accomplished, and the rights reverted to my father.

Around the same time, soon after *Shalako* appeared in bookstores across the country, longtime Paramount star Alan Ladd introduced Louis to a young Englishman named Euan Lloyd. Euan had been a publicist on Ladd's

1953 film *Paratrooper*, and Ladd made the suggestion to producers Irving Allen and Albert "Cubby" Broccoli that Lloyd be allowed to work in a production capacity on their next picture, *The Black Knight*. After a few years of making travel documentaries and assisting Richard Widmark in his 1961 production *The Secret Ways*, Lloyd had finally come to Los Angeles, with the intent of pursuing a career as an independent producer.

What follows are excerpts from a letter Euan wrote to me in 2003 describing the beginning of his friendship with Louis and their eventual business relationship:

> When I finally got to LA . . .
> Alan invited me to his home to
> meet a few friends. Few friends
> indeed!! The house was packed with
> celebrities [. . .] And then, to my
> utter amazement, he brought me
> together with Louis L'Amour. After
> a brief introduction, Alan returned
> to the crowd and I was left with
> Louis . . . for over two hours!

Euan explained that growing up in Depression-era England, he had fallen in love with the film and fiction of the American West and the work of John Wayne, Howard Hawks, George Stevens, and Delmer Daves [a less-remembered but very prolific writer and director]. It had always been Euan's great dream to produce a Western movie.

> As the evening drew to a close
> he [Louis] . . . asked . . . "If

```
you had the choice of any of my
novels . . . which would you
choose?" Instantly, I replied,
SHALAKO. He asked why (although
I am certain he knew what my
answer would be). "Because, as a
European I can relate to that story
and its fascinating bunch of
characters" . . . Your father's
response was short and very sweet.
". . . I'll give you a free option
on SHALAKO for one year. See what
you can do with it. We'll tie up
the details tomorrow."
```

While this is probably a somewhat romanticized version of what really happened, it does catch the flavor of the relationship. Dad and Euan immediately trusted and respected one another, and even if they didn't create the greatest films of the era, it is worthwhile to take a moment and describe exactly what it was they were trying to do.

Euan's goal was to become an *independent* producer. That meant that he believed he had a way to get movies made while bypassing the Hollywood studios, which were still nearly all-powerful. Independence (or some form of autonomy within the labyrinthine power structures of the studios) has long been the holy grail for many a movie producer, but the trade-off is being responsible for many of the jobs the studios do well and efficiently along with the ones they don't. Far too many filmmakers lose sight of this distinction in their desire to go it alone!

With a background in publicity and a rare reputation for integrity, Euan believed he could cobble together enough commitments from bankable movie stars to interest European theater chains and then use *those* contracts to get the bank (or other) loans which would ultimately finance the film. These days this has become the classic model for "independent production," but it is rarely successful on a film-by-film basis, because it is a lot like trying to walk a tightrope while juggling *and* playing the harmonica. Studio-style filmmaking is generally a difficult enough process; adding moving parts by the dozen does not make it any easier.

The term "independent" has meant a lot of different things in Hollywood history, but from the time when Thomas Edison controlled the patents on both cameras and film right through to today, there has always been a filmmaking power structure of some sort that rebellious producers have sought to circumvent. In Euan's day, the studios' power had been compromised by a 1948 court decision that required them to relax control of their theaters. This, along with the popularity of television, caused a slump in ticket sales that lasted into the 1970s.

The first reaction of the Hollywood majors was to go big—they tried to outdo TV with extravagant spectacles. When that proved too costly, the industry veered toward smaller productions, often inspired by the European movies that were becoming more and more common in American theaters. The hope was that if the production costs of an independent film like Euan was planning could be covered by its European release, profits might be found in the theaters of the United States even without significant studio support.

Euan had expertise that uniquely benefited him when it

came to dealing with distributors. He had been a theater
manager and worked with J. Arthur Rank, a pioneering
distributor and owner of a number of British movie studios. He had also been a film industry publicist for,
among many others, Carl Foreman and Samuel Gold-
wyn. While many producers might be experts in shep-
herding a movie through the various phases of physical
production, Euan knew from brutal experience what it
was like to open a film and sell it to an audience. He
knew what theater owners wanted to see in a cast and
what sort of promotional events would give them the
confidence to commit to one project over another.

The deal between Euan Lloyd and my father was
written up not long after Alan Ladd's tragic death in 1964.
Euan was in the midst of finishing a film for the United
Nations and starting *Murderers' Row,* the second install-
ment of a campy spy series starring Dean Martin, but
he took the time to contact director Edward Dmytryk,
a friend from his days with J. Arthur Rank. Dmytryk
agreed to allow Euan to use his name as a prospective
director for *Shalako,* and the two attempted to hash out
a budget that would balance what Euan thought he could
get from distributors with their assessment of what the
production and the cast would cost. Here is Euan in that
same 2003 letter:

> My first ambition, finance wise,
> was to make the picture on a
> $2,000,000 budget. We built a list
> of actors and added their likely
> fees alongside. Not many key
> players would consider SHALAKO at
> the price I could offer. But Eddie

Dmytryk had a strong personal
relationship with Henry Fonda, one
of my favorites. I elected to
pursue that thought, vigorously,
and flew to New York to meet him,
having sent the material ahead. I
was courteously entertained at
breakfast and finally got down to
business. He said the novel was
excellent [. . . and if . . .]
Dmytryk was going to direct he
would do it. I was overjoyed but
was quickly brought to earth when
Mr. Fonda said . . . "I'm afraid
you are in for a long battle with
Hollywood. I am not the flavour
of the month and I doubt very much
if you will get a distribution
deal on my name. But go ahead and
try."

As *Murderers' Row* made its way into postproduction, Euan Lloyd pressed on with what he hoped would soon be his next project:

I engaged the services of a
fiery French sales-agent named
Albert Caraco. . . . He thought the
combination of Henry Fonda and
[actress] Senta Berger plus
Director Edward Dmytryk was
distinctly promising and in double-
quick time [. . .] he obtained

offers to cover two thirds of the budget.

All this seemed to be good news, but in filmmaking it's always that final piece of the plan that is the sticking point. Euan continued:

> Now I badly needed a guarantee from the United States. Almost predictably, my Hollywood contacts responded with a very negative NO to Henry Fonda. [. . .] I was trapped. [. . .] I was fearful that having used Henry Fonda's name I would be faced with a lawsuit if I backed off. Returning to New York to explain my predicament to Henry Fonda, that great man was unmoved by Hollywood's response . . . he smiled and said "But Mr. Lloyd, I DID warn you, didn't I? Don't worry, you go ahead and make SHALAKO without me. And good luck!"

By this time Euan's option with my father was just about over. He carefully explained the situation to both Dad and our agent, Mauri Grashin, fearful that they might have run out of patience. What Euan came quickly to realize was that Dad, having lived on the edges of Hollywood for years, knew the risks and realized there was little that could be done about them. He liked Euan, and that was more than he could say for most of the producers he had done business with. Louis agreed to sign off on options which would carry Euan well into 1967.

Without the star power necessary to lock in any of his theatrical commitments, and concerned, in perfect catch-22 style, that those commitments really wouldn't give him enough money to *afford* a star big enough to satisfy them, Euan set out to see if he could find a way to lower production costs. He also seems to have announced a production date of May of 1967 to the film industry press. Whether this was to instill confidence that the film actually *was* going to be made and could get along without anyone who didn't get aboard, or if it was just a detail made up by an aspiring reporter, is unknown. Very little presented in entertainment news should be accepted without a certain degree of suspicion. Even when not literally made up, rumor is often reported as fact.

Budgetwise, shooting in the United States was considered impossible. So a plan was developed to play the governments of Yugoslavia and Iran against each other. The goal was to get one of them to offer either enough production capacity, bank loans, or cash to make the production possible. On a previous film, Euan had found the government of Iran to be extremely helpful, loaning the movie everything from helicopters to eight hundred soldiers to use as extras. Iran was also the better choice when it came to duplicating the mountains, deserts, and even the towns of New Mexico. The similarity was uncanny. In March of 1967, Euan wrote Louis to bring him up to speed:

```
I am back in Munich after a
hectic weekend in Teheran. . . .
```

I was able to indoctrinate the
Queen, her numerous advisors,
the Governors of three banks (all
Government controlled) and a
prominent film man of their choice
with whom I shall work if the co-
production deal is worked out. As
you would expect the Queen and her
counselors see many built-in
advantages for Iran if a film
industry is developed--with tourist
business to follow. Further, I am
assured that the Shah is fully
aware of the plan and has
encouraged it.

Another reason Iran was looking like the answer (provided they could solve their casting problems and make
a new attempt to raise funds from European and American theater chains) was that Dmytryk was about to
begin *Anzio*, a WWII film shot in Italy. By the time production on that movie wrapped up, they feared conditions in Yugoslavia might be too wintery to work.

Returning to the problem of a star, Dmytryk and Euan
went back through every idea they had come up with
over the preceding year. Here's another excerpt from
Euan's 2003 letter:

My assembly of Possibles and
Probables contained the names of the
Great and the Small. . . . Added in
pencil at the end of the list
was . . . SEAN CONNERY. Eddie

enquired, "Where did he come from?
We've never discussed him." I
explained that some weeks before,
when lunching with Louis L'Amour, I
had remarked that Cubby Broccoli had
yet another huge success with his
latest James Bond release and that
Sean Connery was getting raves.
Louis, half way through a huge
portion of seven-layer-cake,
said . . . "Yes, he's terrific. HE
WOULD SIT WELL IN THE SADDLE!!!"
Eddie asked, "Do you think you can
get him?" "NO," I replied . . . "but
I'll give it a try." I knew Sean's
agent quite well. During an
expensive lunch at the White
Elephant Club in London, the agent
was fascinated by the prospect of
seeing Sean in a Classic Western.
"I like it . . . but Sean is making
a documentary in Glasgow shipyards
and I have instructions not to
disturb him." I pleaded with him to
try. Six weeks later . . . he called
to say Sean would like to meet with
me and Dmytryk.

It didn't hurt that Connery was in the midst of a dis-
pute with Euan's old mentor Cubby Broccoli, producer
of the Bond films. At the time, it no longer looked like
Connery would be doing more of them. On June 12,
1967, we received the following telegram:

```
Dear Louis and Kathy proud and
happy to inform you Sean Connery
will play SHALAKO. . . . Love,
Euan
```

Looking back on it from today's perspective, one would think that landing Sean Connery would cause everything to proceed swimmingly from that point on. But in 1967 things were not nearly so simple. Although the foreign sales agents, led by the indefatigable Albert Caraco, were ecstatic, Euan continued to have trouble in Hollywood:

```
To test the US market I
approached three major studios.
Each of the three studios repeated
the history of Fonda. . . . "Euan,
you must be mad. . . . Connery
hasn't a snowball's chance in hell
after Bond. He's dead meat from now
on." Stalled again, I decided to go
for a major international star to
back up Sean and to increase the
film's potential overseas. I
pursued and got Brigitte
Bardot. . . . Publicity wise, it
was a coup. The duet made front
page news everywhere.
```

The entire reason that Euan wanted to be an independent was to avoid being dictated to by the studios. However, dealing with the distribution side of the business is often just as difficult as playing games with the production offices. There was no question that Connery was one of the hottest and most highly paid actors in the world, but in Hollywood, he was typecast. Nevertheless, even if the American distributors were skeptical, Euan was certain his popularity could stretch beyond the James Bond franchise. He knew he was on the right path, so he doubled down and created what was probably, at least in Europe, the fantasy casting "package" of the decade by signing Bardot.

But the lack of interest from Los Angeles was not the only problem facing Euan Lloyd. The old challenge of balancing the cost of his new cast with what the distributors would be willing to pay had him teetering on the brink of disaster.

> The budget was now $4m. Before Sean would sign his contract I was negotiating on a fee comparable with his Bond price . . . but he hedged and began to harden his stance. Learning from my time as Cubby's PA [production assistant] I decided to go for broke. Sean's highest fee had been $600,000 . . . so I offered his first million dollar deal . . . part cash, part deferred. We closed. Thus, I got one of the biggest stars in the business and Connery was now able to boast about a $1m. salary.

From the perspective of Euan's 2003 letter this makes it seem like the situation was firmly under control, yet back in June of 1967 he had sent the following to Dad's agent:

> Dear Mauri: . . . The two-year-old struggle is going well and I am very close to making a deal. However, to get the man I want I may have to give away my shirt, tie-pin and memories. My car has gone already. I am sure you know how tough it is to put the right kind of deal together in the right way and on your own terms; it's virtually impossible. So it becomes necessary to think about getting as much as possible up front and hope that one's labour of love will eventually pay profits, after many others have collected theirs.

He went on to ask if it would be all right to offer Dad a greater up-front fee (taken out of the film's budget), providing Louis would give up half of his participation in the film's potential profits. From the way this letter is phrased, the suggestion seems to be that the shift would help with Connery's enormous payout, but I also know that if a movie producer goes to a financial institution with theatrical commitments for a certain amount, that institution never hands over the entire figure; the difference is how the bank makes its profit. It also requires a completion bond, which is basically an expensive insurance policy guaranteeing that you will finish the film. At the last moment there are often a good many financial adjustments that need to be made, and everyone involved knows that the filmmaker is over a barrel.

In the end, however, Euan did not let my father down. With a large number of powerful players all lined up ahead of him, Dad's chances of ever getting any money from the film's profits were very low. Doubling his up-front fees, which is the deal Euan was offering, gave him a healthy payday (good but not exceptional for the era) as soon as the film started shooting, and money in hand was money no one could refuse to pay you later on.

Euan was doing no better; besides having sold his car and a mink coat belonging to his wife, his letter to my father from that March reveals:

> I have now spent well over
> $20,000 on the project and
> certainly this will grow before I
> start recovering on completion of
> the deal. . . .

This same letter mentions that Edward Dmytryk had persuaded two young American writers [Hal Hopper and J.J. Griffith] to rewrite the existing Clarke Reynolds screenplay and that he [Dmytryk] was happy with the result. Though I have never checked the film to see if his advice was taken, Louis responded to one of these screenplays (it's unclear which) with the following notes:

NOTES ON SHALAKO SCRIPT:

> p.25: There is no such thing as
> "silver dust" in this sense.

Gold is a heavy metal and when broken from an ore body is washed down stream until the water slows and the gold is then precipitated, falling to the bottom, often behind some obstruction in the stream such as a rock, a sand bar, ect [etc]. Or in the case of placer mining, behind the riffles of a sluice (small wooden cleats across the bottom of the trough). Being heavy, the gold particles will not remain on the surface but will tend to work their way down through the sand until they reach hard-pan, some variety of solid rock. This is not true of silver. And the term "silver dust" was never used in mining or in the west.

p.26: Shalako does not do the Army's dirty work, and he would not admit it if he did. Carrying messages is scarcely that, in any event.

p.33: How did West Point get into this? Anybody can read Jomini, Saxe, ect [etc]. I had read them by the time I was seventeen, and so had my grandfather, who told me about them.

If Shalako becomes a West Point

man you lose the contrast between Irina and himself which is vital. If he attended West Point he is automatically a "gentleman" and therefore on a par with her. The frontiersmen, traveled but rough-hewn presents a nice contrast to the countess. If Shalako attended West Point the contrast is lost.

Why address him as Colonel? It makes no sense whatever, and who ever heard of a colonel carrying messages for the Army, except between generals?

In several places Frederick calls Irina "countess" and he would not do so. He would, being a close friend and a prospective bridegroom, call her Irina or Madame. He would use the title only when introducing her or he might refer to her by title in speaking to another person not the intimate of either.

p.79: Brushing out tracks. This has to be done with care. Burt Lancaster once did this in a picture that was in most respects quite good, but he was shown brushing out tracks with all the vigor of a woman on a dirty floor.

A tracker does not necessarily

look for <u>tracks</u>, as such. He
watches for anything disturbed,
anything out of context. The marks
of such brushing would be even more
obvious than the tracks because of
the effort made to conceal them. If
tracks are brushed out they should
be brushed with feather-like
strokes and then sand held up and
released from the hand to settle
naturally over the tracks. Or marks
of brushing.

Tracks or trail indications are
rarely obvious. A man following
such a trail would rarely leave the
saddle. If he did he would walk
ahead, leading his horse and
studying the ground as he moves.
Sometimes indications are many
yards apart. A bruised plant or
leaf here, a white scratch of a
horse-shoe on rock there, or a
pebble kicked out of place. In
hard-packed clay a pebble will
often lie in a socket, and when
kicked out will roll to one side.

Reservation boundaries meant
nothing at all to a war party of
Indians. They would cross them
without a thought.

One item of importance; <u>there was
no reason why an Army unit could
not come on a reservation</u>. They

often did, and I [could] quote fifty
instances of it. The Indians rarely
created trouble on the reservation,
although there were cases of it.
Trouble usually developed when
Indians left the reservation, and
wild Apaches were forever trying to
get them to leave.

Army units were often permanently
camped on reservations.

The cactus you want is the
bisnaga, or barrel cactus. It is a
short, stubby cactus with many
spines. It has no arms or branches,
and many are no bigger around or
taller than a common pail or water-
bucket. I would say that a barrel
cactus more then eighteen inches in
circumference would be the exception
although I have seen them up to
two feet across. They rarely run to
six feet high, and most that I have
seen run from two to four feet.

There is a tendency to grow
toward the most intense light so
such a cactus is often leaning
somewhat. The juice is strictly for
emergencies, slimy and somewhat
alkaline but it is wet and it will
save life and has done so many
times.

The cactus must be cut into with
a knife (preferably a long blade

because of the spines) or it can be
broken open on the top with rocks
or even a strong stick. The cactus
stores water and the pulp inside is
juicy. Jack rabbits, wild burros
and mountain sheep occasionally eat
the flesh to get the moisture. It
definitely could be used as it is
in the script.

They are shaped much like the
stump of a moderately sized tree.

Hope this is of some help, and
the best of luck, always . . .

Sincerely,
Louis L'Amour

It's not at all common for a novelist to be invited to
comment on a movie script, or even to be sent a copy.
Once the deal for the rights is made the writer of a book
is rarely involved, consulted, or even notified of anything
except the film's completion. Even *screenwriters* are
often persona non grata on the set.

It is interesting to see that Louis and Euan had a different dynamic than was typical in Hollywood: Euan
discussed all of the broad strokes with Dad, and Dad
was very comfortable letting Euan do what he needed to
in order to get the job done. Dad probably could have
gotten more involved with the making of Euan's films if
he'd wanted to, but all he really wanted was to write
whatever was on his mind at the moment. He knew that
he didn't have the know-how to debate the finer points
of filmmaking and that the details of production could

quickly draw you down a rat hole of impossible compromises and industry politics. As in this case, if he was allowed a say he typically kept his commentary limited to practical details rather than trying to second-guess the filmmaker's take on the story as a whole. He had already done his version; the only way forward was to keep from looking back.

With a script in hand and a cast and distribution plan having come together within just a few weeks, the pressure was on to make use of the opportunity before it began to disappear. The slowly evolving plans for shooting in Iran were scrapped, and the possibility of working in Mexico was explored, then also ditched because of the likelihood of a strike. Ultimately, a decision to shoot in the Almeria region of Spain was made.

The year 1967 ended with Euan scrambling to assemble a cast and crew, many of whom were drawn from earlier films he had been involved with and from veterans of Broccoli's Bond franchise. Principal photography began in the first week of 1968. The struggle to find a way to produce *Shalako* as a truly independent motion picture had finally given way to its actual production.

I have very little information about the filming of the movie except for a February letter from Euan saying that all was going well. On March 23, the film wrapped, and by July Euan was well into the details of the distribution plan:

Dear Louis (and all),

. . . I am just back from Munich after several days of meetings and

activity on SHALAKO. I am pleased
to say the world premiere will be
in Munich on September 26th with
59 theatres across Germany and
Austria following on the 27th. It's
the best release pattern I could
possibly hope for--even better than
the Bond plan. . . . America is
presently set for October 10th, in
about 350 theatres, and their plan
looks promising too. But I will
have to sit on them, I'm sure, and
therefore expect to be in New York
about September 1st and then
onwards West! So don't expect me
before September 5th or so.

As the process of cutting the film wound down, Euan
had a sudden onset of cold feet, regarding the same
subject that had disturbed the "Old Buckaroos" of the
Western Writers of America: the question of whether au-
diences could accept the idea of Europeans in America
acting like Europeans on an African safari. In response,
Dad copied off a good deal of the same information he
had sent the WWA, and the company shooting *Shalako*'s
credits turned it into a historical note to be tacked onto
the film.

These efforts didn't solve the problem, at least not
completely. The reviews were fairly mixed, though in the
case of the bad ones Louis's novel was usually exempted
from criticism. But soon after the American premiere in
San Francisco on October 8, a review again slammed the

premise as being "improbable," using the same word as the WWA.

My father's response was nearly identical to his earlier one. As he was careful to point out, it was completely legitimate to criticize the creative qualities of the story—he was critical of it himself—but the film's premise was solid.

The 1960s was a time when people's perceptions were being expanded in a great many ways. Dad welcomed the opportunity to evolve beyond the typical restrictions of the genre; however, some seemed to have a hard time accepting that the Western genre could withstand any change at all. Strangely, many of those complaints came from the more intellectual types, like writers and critics. I do not remember any fan mail from an average reader complaining about the "improbabilities" of *Shalako*.

The European reaction to the film was generally better than the American. At the premiere in Munich, crazed fans overturned the car that Brigitte Bardot and Steven Boyd (her *Shalako* costar and ex-lover) arrived in. Not only were the reviews considerably more positive, but the film seemed to be making money.

In the years following its release, stories varied wildly about *Shalako*'s financial success, but for the most part it came down to which side of the Atlantic Ocean you were on. Echoing the "You can't have Europeans in the West" controversy, to this day people connected to the American distribution of *Shalako* will argue that making a European the star of a Western is asking for trouble. That's ridiculous, of course, but the powers that be in the publishing industry once said that a guy with a foreign-sounding name like "Louis L'Amour" could never be a Western writer!

Most of the time movie producers are notorious for promising the moon and delivering a slightly shiny pebble. And at some point in the process, Euan had sold my parents on the prestigious presentation that *Shalako* would receive when it premiered in the British Isles. He even suggested that he would arrange for a Gala Royal Premiere at the Variety Club in London and that they would be able to attend, all expenses paid.

Longtime veterans of Hollywood hype, Mom and Dad believed very little of this, or assumed it was just a case of a producer being carried away with his own salesmanship and suffering delusions of grandeur. Regardless, they were impressed with how much Euan had kept them in the loop and how forthright he had been about the difficulties he'd had pulling the financial package together.

It was his personal style and integrity that impressed them most of all. In Hollywood, manipulation is compulsively practiced, and many movie types don't seem to consider something a success unless it has involved at least a bit of a con. My parents were slowly learning that this was in no way true of their new friend. A few years ago a documentary was made about the life and career of Euan Lloyd; it was appropriately titled *The Last of the Gentleman Producers*.

When it came to the rollout of the film in the United Kingdom, Euan was as good as his word. A star-studded Royal Premiere with Princess Margaret and her husband, Lord Snowdon, in attendance went off without a hitch, as did a second premiere in Glasgow. My parents were deeply impressed by the way everything was managed, by both the film's publicity department and my father's British publisher, Corgi. Here is an excerpt from a letter Dad wrote to his sister in December of 1968 describing the details of the trip:

It was a great experience, furst [first] to last, all our expenses paid, and nothing at all to worry about. One can easily see how easy it is to be spoiled: people to meet us at every point, limousines waiting, taken right through customs without so much as stopping or answering even one question, and the V.I.P. treatment everywhere. Every smallest detail paid for by the film, laundry, cleaning, food, etc.

We had a smooth, easy flight by way of Iceland, and landed in England where Euan met us with a couple of old hands at the game from the distributor of the film in England, and from that moment on, everything was done for us.

In fact, the promotional aspects of the trip were so well handled that the entire family returned to England the following summer. We took in the sights while Dad did research and made the rounds of speaking and autographing engagements. In the end we were presented with a huge scrapbook of all of Louis's events. My mother, who often functioned as Dad's agent, used this tome to impress the Bantam executives in New York—until that time they had done next to nothing to help publicize my father's work. The example set by the British film and publishing industry on these two trips changed the way Louis L'Amour was presented to the public for the next twenty years.

I believe the last time I saw Euan was in London around 2004. Though he was over eighty, I would have recognized him anywhere. Of course, he had aged since I'd first met him as a child, but nowhere near as much as one might have expected. He regaled me with stories about the film business in England and Hollywood, films he had worked on and people he had known. Besides his telling an amusing story about Sean Connery crashing on his couch and spending a couple of days quietly reading poetry, the men he spoke most warmly about were my father and Alan Ladd.

I can't remember any particular quote from our conversation, but there is a bit from that letter my father wrote his sister just after returning from England that kind of sums things up:

> Euan (Lloyd) did not forget anybody. John Haskell, who is married to Dorothy Manners, introduced Euan to Alan Ladd, who gave Euan his best leg up. They talked some, and later when British films wanted Alan to do a picture Alan told them all right, he would do it if they would give Euan a job. . . . (Alan was a guy who did many fine things very much that

way, sort of off-hand and without any talk about it.) Later, of course, it was Alan who introduced Euan to me, so his shadow was behind the whole thing. Euan wanted to dedicate the picture to Alan, but Sean's agent objected, for some incomprehensible reason.

Beau L'Amour
December 2018

ABOUT LOUIS L'AMOUR

*"I think of myself in the oral tradition—
as a troubadour, a village taleteller, the man
in the shadows of the campfire. That's the way
I'd like to be remembered—as a storyteller.
A good storyteller."*

IT IS DOUBTFUL that any author could be as at
home in the world re-created in his novels as Louis
Dearborn L'Amour. Not only could he physically fill the
boots of the rugged characters he wrote about, but he
literally "walked the land my characters walk." His personal experiences as well as his lifelong devotion to historical research combined to give Mr. L'Amour the
unique knowledge and understanding of people, events,
and the challenge of the American frontier that became
the hallmarks of his popularity.

As a boy growing up in Jamestown, North Dakota,
he absorbed all he could about his family's frontier heri-
tage, including the story of his great-grandfather who
was scalped by Sioux warriors.

Spurred by an eager curiosity and desire to broaden
his horizons, Mr. L'Amour left home at the age of fifteen
and enjoyed a wide variety of jobs, including seaman,
lumberjack, elephant handler, skinner of dead cattle,
miner, and an officer in the transportation corps during
World War II. He was a voracious reader and collector

of books. His personal library contained 17,000 volumes.

Mr. L'Amour "wanted to write almost from the time I could talk." After developing a widespread following for his many frontier and adventure stories written for fiction magazines, Mr. L'Amour published his first full-length novel, *Hondo,* in the United States in 1953. Every one of his more than 120 books is in print; there are more than 300 million copies of his books in print worldwide, making him one of the bestselling authors in modern literary history. His books have been translated into twenty languages, and more than forty-five of his novels and stories have been made into feature films and television movies.

His hardcover bestsellers include *The Lonesome Gods, The Walking Drum* (his twelfth-century historical novel), *Jubal Sackett, Last of the Breed,* and *The Haunted Mesa.* His memoir, *Education of a Wandering Man,* was a leading bestseller in 1989. Audio dramatizations and adaptations of many L'Amour stories are available from Random House Audio.

The recipient of many great honors and awards, in 1983 Mr. L'Amour became the first novelist ever to be awarded the Congressional Gold Medal by the United States Congress in honor of his life's work. In 1984 he was also awarded the Medal of Freedom by President Reagan.

Louis L'Amour died on June 10, 1988.